Learning English

by Rachid al-Daif

translated by Paula and Adnan Haydar

ARABIA BOOKS
www.arabia-books.com

First published in Great Britain in 2009 by

ARABIA BOOKS
70 Cadogan Place
London SW1X 9AH
www.arabia-books.com

First published in 2007 by

INTERLINK BOOKS
An imprint of the Interlink Publishing Group, Inc.
www.interlinkbooks.com

ISBN 978-1-906697-21-1

Printed in Great Britain by J. F. Print Ltd, Sparkford

CONDITIONS OF SALE

Works available in English by Rachid al-Daif:

Dear Mr. Kawabata
Passage to Dusk
This Side of Innocence

T hat was all I needed. To hear the news of my father's murder by chance! Two whole days after it happened. After his funeral and after his burial were already over!

He was killed at noon on Saturday, buried Sunday afternoon, and I didn't hear about any of it until noon on Monday.

I was in Beirut, at the Café de Paris as I usually am every day at noon. A friend, who was sitting beside me, suddenly stopped reading his newspaper to ask me with shock who Hamad D. was in relation to me.

"My father," I said, and he was even more shocked. Then, with a mechanical motion, he handed me the paper to read. The item appeared in the daily police record. A few terse words in tiny print like some bit of scattered news hardly worth mention:

TEL SQUARE, ZGHARTA, shortly after
noon Saturday, Hamad D. (age 60) was
murdered, a case of blood revenge.

I stood up from my chair like a madman.

"Really?" I exclaimed.

When my friend saw how upset I was, he tried to make me feel better by saying, "Couldn't there be someone else with that name?"

I didn't answer. I appeared even more shocked and upset, so my friend said, as if trying to apologize for the unintentional damage he had caused me, "Are you sure he's your father?"

Oh God!

He killed me with that question. He blew my mind with that question.

Could he have felt something, or sensed something, even though he had absolutely no idea? He knew no more about me than what any other coffee shop acquaintance knew. Or had he sensed certain reverberations about me and repressed them all these years only to have them suddenly leak out now from the shock?

No!

If he knew something or had suspicions, then he wouldn't have asked me that question, because coming from someone who had knowledge about such matters (particularly such matters) such a question would lead to very serious consequences.

(Oh God! Innocence and lack of knowledge can cause so much harm!)

But what should my friend matter to me now? Whether he knew something or not, it didn't change the fact of what had happened, and the fact was my father was murdered, and even more importantly, he was given a funeral and was buried in my absence and without my knowledge.

How could that possibly be?

Had my uncles seen in my father's murder a golden opportunity to take revenge on my mother, and on me, too? Or had they all been in on the plan, my mother and my uncles, to take revenge on me in this cruel manner? Otherwise, how could it be?

How could no one have told me? When I'm right here in Beirut, a mere phone call away from Zgharta, or an hour by car on a Saturday afternoon when the traffic to Beirut is light? There is not a single means of communication available in Lebanon that I'm not registered for. I have a regular phone line at my house, and a cell phone— and let me point out that I was one of the first people to register for that cell phone, a good six months before cell phones came into common use in 1995. And I have Internet access, too, and love everything to do with computers and anything digital; I'm enchanted by all of that. I sometimes spend all my monthly savings on it. The easiest thing in the world is to get in touch with me, easier than reaching the absolute majority of people, including the privileged, the well-to-do, and even the ruling class who hold the country's future in their hands. So how come I wasn't informed?

Furthermore, I left my house hardly at all those two days, not at night or during the day, and when I did leave for a couple of hours I left my answering machine on and I know it was working, because several messages were left on it Saturday and Sunday and I listened to them without any problem.

So how could this be?

Had time run its course all these years just to finally come around and prove that those nightmares I lived in fear of, especially in my early youth and adolescence, actually had a basis? Were actually based in fact? Could it be that what I thought were just "things" everyone else forgot about, even if I continued to struggle with them alone, were actually on the minds of everyone around me, especially my uncles?

"Calm down, Rashid!" I said. There's no reason to assume the worst. Certainly it is incredible for your father to be murdered and for no one to inform you, but that's all it is: your father was murdered and no one told you. Nothing more, nothing less. It's not revenge, or banishment, or a disowning. So don't go opening up closed cases no one cares about anymore but you—there is nothing that merits doing that. Your friend's question had to do with the uncomfortable situation he found himself in; he did not mean anything by it. He asked you that question, not because he wanted to know if you were sure the man who was murdered was really your father, but to apologize for the pain he had caused you, and to convey his wish that the news wasn't true, that it wasn't your father who had been killed. His question was an attempt to get out of a predicament he suddenly found himself in involuntarily and unknowingly. It was not a direct result of your not having been informed about the incident, and the relationship between that and whether your father is really your father. Moreover, he did not deduce whatsoever from the appearance of the news item or from your reaction to it that your mother and your uncles did not inform you of your father's murder, for there was nothing that inferred such a deduction. The only thing a person could possibly deduce was that your father was murdered and you didn't know. That's all, so calm down!

Take it easy. Get a grip on yourself, because the victim was your father, and the motive was revenge, and that gives rise to consequences, and you know very well what they are.

I was in complete shock.

It's no simple matter to lose your father, but it's even worse for him to be murdered, and then for you to find out about it in this way—in a coffee shop, by chance. I tried to get hold of myself but the shock and surprise were stronger than I was, and I was overcome. My usually calm and quiet nature did not succeed in stopping the feeling that my head was spinning around a hundred revolutions per minute. It was as if my brain had multiplied and now I had many brains, each one working independently and in a different direction. It was as if the world had lost consciousness, or simply disappeared.

From the coffee shop to my house I walked on a sidewalk that had disappeared, to a place that had disappeared, in the middle of a day that had disappeared, amidst human beings who had disappeared and cars that had disappeared. The clamor was without sound, and sound itself had no chord to sound on.

Some sort of instinct, whose nature I cannot explain, led me to my house.

That's why the first thing I had to do was take a tranquil-izer to help me get back in control and consequently back home right away so I could make some necessary phone calls before heading to Zgharta without delay. Tranquilizers are a sort of habit of mine, but only in very stressful situations. I'm not addicted to them—I just use them when I need them is all, which is not very often, only a few times in a whole year.

On my way from the café I stopped at a drugstore located at the entrance to the building where I live and bought some low-strength Ativan (one milligram). And I asked the young pharmacist for a glass of water, too. That confused her, as she knew I lived in the same building. No doubt she wondered about this need of mine that was so urgent I couldn't bear a few more seconds, which was the amount of time it would take to go up the few flights of stairs to my apartment. But after some hesitation she fulfilled my request. I took one pill and left.

I'm actually a very calm man by nature, with or without the tranquilizer that is, but with it, the situation would be better, because dealing with the matter currently at hand required much concentration.

I was surprised to find the contents of my apartment out of their usual state; they were dead. I mean, they were solid blocks, as if my dead father had somehow infected them and transformed them. Only a dead father could possibly leave that kind of effect, and only my dead father could have done that to the things in my house. The way I felt toward the things in my apartment seemed to me to confirm his death, or rather to confirm the feeling of kinship toward him I held deep inside. For, despite everything, he was my father, and I was his son, his flesh and blood.

I headed directly for the phone. There was a message on the answering machine (it was working!) so I listened to it before calling our house in Zgharta. I thought the message might be from there, from Zgharta, but it was from my girlfriend, Salwa, and it consisted of one short sentence that contained the entire history of our relationship, with all its chronic problems: "It's me, Salwa!"

And that meant, "I'm at home and I want and am able to come over and I'm waiting for you to call me so I can come, and if you don't you'll hurt my feelings and embarrass me in front of my mother who is always chiding me and saying that I'm always the one calling you and you hardly ever call me, which means to her that I'm 'chasing you and you don't want me.'"

After listening to that message, which was from Salwa and not from anyone in my family, I immediately plugged my cell phone into the charger and turned it on so all the means of communication I had would be in perfect running condition. That would prevent giving anyone an excuse to claim he or she couldn't get hold of me. Because what was going on was serious, very serious. That I realized right away, without any introductions, explanations, or deductions. No, by a natural instinct inside of me, in my flesh and bones and blood. I was after all a child of that town, of that particular town, not the child of any other city or region in Lebanon or elsewhere in the Arab world, and certainly not of New York or anywhere else in the West where blood revenge, they say, has completely disappeared from their customs and no one encounters it anymore. Actually, family ties there have loosened, most people would agree. But I am from that town that has been notorious for a half century or more for its blood-revenge customs, like those of the pre-Islamic tribes of the Arabian Peninsula where blood revenge was a kind of religious duty. To a large extent, those same customs are still being preserved with no significant modifications or substitutions, as if there were something about them that was even stronger than the passing of years and centuries, as if they were of a different nature than years and centuries, and time was incapable of having any effect on them. People still believe that their fallen relative cannot rest in his grave until his blood is avenged, and they still swear against enjoying any of life's pleasures until their lost one is avenged.

Some won't even receive the body until the victim has been avenged, forcing the men of religion to step in and the other civil authorities, too, with methods they know well, methods that will move things along. Some of these people receive the body but won't bury it before the victim has been avenged, while some bury the body temporarily and then transfer it to its final resting place once vengeance has extinguished the flames of the loved one's blood.

And the women still bury themselves in black and stop taking care of themselves for long periods, sometimes until the blood revenge has been taken.

True, incidences of blood revenge have decreased and are no longer carried out in the same manner as in the past. But for the killer to remain on the face of the earth, enjoying sunlight and fresh air, is still absolutely impossible for them to put up with. And they still don't believe in any other form of justice in this matter but the justice they take into their own hands and according to the whims of their unwritten laws.

What has changed today about their customs touches on the form but not the essence. They used to fight each other more, now they fight less; they used to fight with daggers or swords, now they fight with guns; they used to travel on mule or horse back, now they travel in cars; and the compensation used to be an eye, now it's money.

Yet despite that!

Yet despite all that, no one called to tell me about my father's murder, and I didn't find out about it except by chance, two whole days later, after his funeral and burial.

So what is it all about? And what sinister scheme lies behind this behavior?

What if chance had turned things the opposite way and I never found out about it? Would I have remained ignorant of the fact that my father had been murdered less than a hundred kilometers from where I live, while at the same time people living in the States knew about it, and people living in Australia knew about it, and people in South America and Africa? I might have gotten sympathy cards from Zghartans scattered on all those continents, via the Internet, as I did eventually find later that evening when I opened my e-mail. And none of the letters clarify anything I need to know. All they offer are words of sympathy and advice. "Take it easy," and "Be patient," in a mixture of English, French, and Arabic written in Latin script (*Rooq*! *Tawwil balak*!) (Calm down! Be patient!) And there were a few with offers to help me take revenge.

It isn't just a matter of not having been informed, and there is much more to it than just forgetfulness or negligence. Behind it is a clear attempt to cause serious harm and injury, the kind after which you can't be hurt any more. What lies behind it is of utmost seriousness. Behind it is nothing less than an assassination attempt. Yes, an assassination attempt.

Did they want to say to me, "If you really and truly are the son of our brother, then go ahead! Avenge your father!"

But then again, I must reflect before reaching any conclusions. I decided to call our house in Zgharta right away in order to talk to my mother and ask her some questions that might clarify things. I should also tell her I am coming. It is absolutely necessary to call before heading there so I would be traveling in daylight, not total darkness. There is no wisdom at all in going before calling. Right now patience is a virtue. What happened happened, and hours of waiting, or even a night of waiting, will not change that in any way. But no one answered. I let the phone ring many times, but to no avail. I thought that maybe I'd dialed one of the numbers incorrectly because of the state of shock I was in, or maybe they moved the phone to another place away from where they were receiving condolences. I decided to wait a little while before trying again.

But then, while I was waiting to try calling our house in Zgharta again, I started wondering. What do I have to do with those people anyway? What relationship do I have to them, what connects me to them? And I thought that they, too, must be feeling this estrangement from me, and that was why they hadn't called me. That was quite understandable. Natural, in fact. They really meant something to me, but in a former life. I suddenly felt like I had entered another person's skin and some force was hurling me now once again into a matter that did not concern me. *Those things don't concern me anymore.* They no longer relate to me, are no longer of my world, no longer suit me, for I am from a different time, and my world is now another world that has no connection to that world I was raised in, that world that seems like some other life, other than the one I am living. *Une vie anterieure*, as they say in French. I am happy in this milieu I am living in, at this Lebanese University where I work as a professor in the department of Arabic language and literature, in the College of Arts and Sciences, earning a salary that allows me, despite all the inflation and over-pricing and everything related to that, to have a house (old rent of course!) in an upper-class neighborhood in Beirut near Hamra and near the luxurious Bristol Hotel, in close proximity to the house of the Prime Minister Mr. Rafiq al-Hariri, one of the richest men in the world.

And I'm a divorced man now, after having been married to a French woman I met in Paris while studying for my Ph.D. in Arabic literature. She lives there now, and I don't hear anything from her that can irritate me, nor does she get any irritating news from me. (Maybe that was one of the benefits of marrying a foreigner.) I have one daughter from her who's "all grown up." (Fortunately we don't have a son, for a son is more concerned with his father's history, whereas a daughter melts into her husband's family.) She's a university student now in Paris close to graduating and has a grant that, for the most part, allows her to get by without having to ask me for help. We have a very good relationship. It's been some time now since I've gotten through the painful problems related to the divorce, and my emotions have finally settled into perfect calm, wisdom, and reflection.

I have a girlfriend, also divorced, who lives with her parents and has no children. We have no problem with each other at all; we are in perfect harmony. She doesn't want to get married again, as she has stated to me many times (especially at the beginning of our relationship), and I feel the same, maybe more so. I have no desire at all to get married again. She possesses a small fortune which consists of a number of apartments in Beirut that she rents at the new legal rates, which bring in roughly two thousand American dollars a month—enough for her to live very comfortably without working. She is always praising her luck and expressing her joy at not having to work to live, because she doesn't like working. I spend sweet and happy times with her, especially since she is quite submissive in bed. I discovered with her that I like this type of submissive woman, and I discovered I have a bit of Pharaonic blood in me, which shows itself when given a chance. I discovered with her that I love to be a master in the dark. Indeed, I discovered it is an intense pleasure of mine. And it seems (so far) that she is happy being the way I like her, and always gives me the impression that she is that way by nature and doesn't just act that way for me. The one problem we have is that she is not free to go out whenever she wants from her parents' house where she has lived since her divorce. Her mother always waits up for her and won't sleep until her daughter gets home, and if she's late she opens the door and says, "God created the night for sleeping!" (Her father doesn't interfere in the matter; he leaves her mother to govern the situation with her expertise.) I prefer a woman to be more *disponibilité*, but this is our culture and there's no choice but to behave according to what the circumstances allow. Make do with what you've got, the saying goes.

I'm happy to be known among people as being calm, contemplative, and wise, and more than that, I'm self-sufficient and in no dire need of anything.

And I'm a contemporary person. I wear little round "retro look" glasses, the look of an educated Parisian who has witnessed the events of the student movement of 1968 in France. (I can imagine myself avenging my father wearing these glasses!) I write, read, and speak French fluently, but I have one impediment—*culturellement parlant*—I don't know English. It's an impediment that surfaced only recently, just a few years ago, really. Before that we didn't need English at all—myself and many friends of mine—in order to practice our modernity, our revolutionary nature, and our struggle at all levels—politically, socially, or in terms of making demands and so on. French was sufficient. We were perfectly content and satisfied with it. Actually English was the impediment that did not allow its speakers to advance. English (i.e., the language of America) was the language of the enemy, the language of exploitation, hegemony, arrogance, superficial thinking, pragmatism. And it was the language of money and trade, not the language of subtleties of thinking, not the language of the future, or equality, or social justice, not the language of the theory that leads to something, not the language of profound consciousness. French was the language of these fine values, and we were comfortable using it to organize history and our policies concerning history, and comfortable strengthening our grasp of it so as not to let it stagnate, or head in a direction we did not want it to go. But today I am trying to make up for my deficiency—not knowing English that is—by teaching it to myself. Sometimes my girlfriend, who is fluent in both languages—French and English—perfectly fluent, helps me. Unfortunately, though, the fruits are not equivalent to the labor, and the damage comes from forgetfulness. I forget today what I learned yesterday.

I can't bear not to be contemporary. I have always been contemporary and up-to-date. I was for the progressive Arab liberation movement. I was for the modern Arabic poem and modern Arabic poetry. I was for Marxism and I mastered French. In literary criticism I was a structuralist, and now I follow what is called post-modernism. I bought an extremely advanced computer, and now I use the Internet, and of course I have e-mail.

I can't bear not to be contemporary.

I interpret that as not being able to bear getting old. Modern digital technology, compared to the previous approaches, shortens time and distance, giving a person the impression that he or she has conquered time and place, making him or her God-like. It is indeed the beautiful illusion of immortality. That is how I interpret my love and excitement for the digital world.

I quit smoking, too, which is a very modern stand to take. Post-modern, in fact. And I watch my weight so I don't get any fatter than I should or than what's prescribed in the American magazines I read in translation. And I have precautionary medical tests run and observe carefully any changes in my skin—facial complexion especially— immediately removing anything that might happen to appear on it that should not be there.

I am a real man, ever since the war ended. In particular, I love life and love to enjoy life. (By the war I mean the war that took place in Lebanon between 1975 and 1990.) I am a man who is happy to have accumulated the difficult experiences I lived through during that cursed war. Now I am exceedingly happy when I have an opportunity to talk about them. How often I dreamed of that war ending without my getting killed in it so that I could be one of those who "lived through the war" and "tasted its bitterness." How wonderful for a person to accumulate experiences of such gravity.

That war ended and I felt with its end that I was born again, as if a new life had been granted to me. So why, then? Why?

What does fate want from me? Why doesn't it let me enjoy this new life, or at least what's left of it, especially since I've "paid my dues" and lived through despair, like so many Lebanese? I lived through grief, oppression, danger, degradation, and everything a person can possibly live through during a war. So what do my uncles and my mother want from me now? Why are they opening pages that were shut so long ago? Indeed, why did they want those nightmares that haunted my childhood to come back to haunt me again? Do they realize what they are doing? What can they possibly profit from it?

I am a calm man by nature, and I like this about myself.

I dream of organizing my time as I please. I love hearing about the Egyptian writer Naguib Mahfouz, recipient of the Nobel Prize for Literature, and the orderliness of his life. I always attribute that to the regularity of life in big and ancient cities like Cairo. I also love the line in Rachid al-Daif's first book of poetry, *When the Sword Descended upon Summer*:

> When at summer's end the first rain falls
> My soul assures itself of the orderly passage of the seasons

When I read it I feel as if I'm sitting in the evening in front of the fireplace in winter, safe and warm, while outside the storms roar their madness.

I have always envied Naguib Mahfouz for his stable city of Cairo, in contrast with Beirut, the city of unrest. But at the end of the war I consoled myself that now I could live a stable life in Beirut, because a new war in Lebanon would not break out—if one broke out at all— for many years. Ten, twenty, or more, judging by the intervals between past wars.

I am a calm man by nature, and this calm state I am in now is not haphazard or coincidental, even if it is due to the tranquilizer I took (perfect dose!) for reasons I hope are temporary.

Right now I am under the influence of the tranquilizer. Tranquilizers were something I turned to during the war in Beirut when there was shelling and kidnapping and the worst battles were taking place, whereas other people turned to drinking or gambling or both. So now, because of the pill I took, everything seems bland to me, but I prefer that a thousand times over behaving nervously and recklessly.

I am no longer part of that world my uncles and my mother live in. What is there to make me part of them? Nothing! Nothing but some obscure something, inside me, some obscurity I don't know what to name. But this something is faint, and I can forget it and consider it non-existent. I can disown it.

Disown it!

I can decide right now to disown everything. My father's inheritance and his blood. And his name, too. Yes, his name that I inherited from him. He's nothing but a murderer who went unpunished for his crime because of the power and sway held by his family. He killed the husband of the woman he repeatedly forced to have intimate relations with him, and then just left her to her fate and never asked once what happened to her afterward. I'll name myself something else. I'll name myself whatever I want. I'll name myself some number I choose out of all the numbers. A number will be enough, because all anyone knows me by are my acts and nothing else, my behavior and treatment of others, that's all, so what use is my name to me? What does it get me but a strew of viruses that cling to me and can't be shaken off or dispersed? A name that elicits that megalomania-stricken clan that cannot be contained. A name that keeps me a stranger in this place, this place that knows nothing but what it is accustomed to, and so I am forced to either join forces with it or make enemies with it, or else all the doors will be slammed shut in my face and I'll die from exasperation or agony or torment. I'll disown it then, and stay here in Beirut, never visit Zgharta ever again, never step foot in it again, as they say. *But WAIT! WAIT JUST ONE MINUTE!* (As they say in American movies in these kinds of situations.) None of this changes anything at all about the reality of the situation, nor does it change the nature of the problem, which remains as it is, complete and sufficient, unflagging and unabating. My father was murdered and no one informed me; indeed two whole days have passed since it happened. There is nothing preventing his enemies from killing me if they feel they should, for as his only son I am the primary target for revenge. I am his only son, no matter what, and no matter what my mother always liked to say. (My mother used to respond with such bitter answers, in order to curtail my curiosity about the reasons behind my having remained an only child with no brothers or sisters. She would answer with severe abruptness, "What for?" She used to avoid answering by inserting that bitterness into her reply. And she also used it when answering with the question, "Where are we going to get children from?" Didn't my mother know where children came from? Where did she get me from, then? How did she get me? Wasn't it by getting into bed with my father with some degree of affection?)

They did not inform me of my father's murder and I am the person the most affected by it, the one in most danger—danger of being killed in all this mess, which is a possibility I should not rule out at all, and which I will take every precaution against. No one knows how blood-revenge incidents will be played out, or what they will lead to. Truly, if the killer is extremely careful, to the point of being afflicted with caution, I mean sick with it as sometimes happens, then he might kill those people who are closest to his target—his victim—in order to rid himself of an archenemy. The cautious murderer dreams of wiping out all of his victim's relatives.

I imagine another scenario. My paternal uncles are unable to kill my father's assailant, or whomever they believe to be the mastermind. So they proceed to hunt down the nearest relative and the one most assured that he had nothing to do with the murder, because that makes him an easy target. And thus they would also give the others a reason to feel at ease while the real killer gets away. Then "all hell breaks loose" and vengeance turns into a race for the easiest victory. For you see, a wounded man doesn't hesitate to attack the first victim his hand can reach. Blood revenge prefers the immediate. And I am an easy target, the easiest possible, in fact. I live in Beirut where I have no neighborhood where I can feel safe within its boundaries, as in Zgharta. Here in Beirut I have no choice but to live my life as do hundreds of thousands of other people, by which I mean I can't watch everybody the way families do in Zgharta in their own neighborhoods. And I can't take precautions against everyone or ask questions about new and strange faces I come upon every day, or approach people I'm suspicious about and ask them what they are doing here, and so on. That is just not possible, and that is why I am easy prey. And when I say that, it is not as if I am deciding such a thing, or making it up, but rather I am merely stating the simple fact of a reality I am part of.

And Zgharta isn't so far away from Beirut anymore, the way it was decades ago. Today Lebanon is more like one city; indeed the whole world has become like one big city. And they didn't tell me!

Oh God!

I am such an idealistic dreamer to think that I might claim I don't belong to that world—their world! But that wasn't a dream, it was a feeling.

It was a feeling I felt deep down inside, that this world—their world—belonged to a previous life I might have lived once upon a time but which no longer concerned me.

At any rate, that feeling didn't last very long—*et pour cause*—because it's a feeling that can't possibly last long at all, because I am in the heart of the event, like it or not. No, I am the event itself and cannot escape it. I have to deal with it. I compare my situation to that of a person at the onset of some sickness, when he or she says, "No big deal!" but then doesn't waste one second getting medical attention until he or she is cured. So that feeling didn't last but a fleeting period of time after which the atmosphere became recharged with anxiety and burning questions and I became obsessed to the point of madness with the question, *How could no one have told me?*

Why?

Did something happen to the answering machine, causing it not to work at the time—the time one of them called to tell me—like a dip in the flow of electricity for example, the moment the machine needed to work? Did they try to leave a message but couldn't figure out how, being so unfamiliar with such things? But I didn't notice any blank messages in which the machine starts to record but nothing gets left on it, which happens sometimes because lots of people don't like leaving their voices recorded on answering machines for a thousand different reasons. Or because lots of people still aren't used to answering machines, or don't know how to leave a message on one.

Had they sent someone from Zgharta to tell me and take me with him but he got lost on the way to my house? Or had he been able to find the house but then when he didn't find me at home he left a note on the door telling me to call him right away at some phone number, cellular or land line, but the paper got lost the way it does from time to time when friends who stop by unexpectedly leave a note on my apartment door but then I don't find it, as if someone liked to go around tearing these notes off my door. And I always suspect the concierge when this happens, and it very well might be the concierge who did it this time, because he mops the stairs on Saturday or Sunday, once or sometimes twice a month, and I did notice the stairs had been mopped last Sunday, or Saturday. So I ran down to the ground floor and knocked on the concierge's door. His wife, who always helps him mop the floor, answered, so I asked her if they had seen a note for me stuck to my apartment door. "No, no. We don't touch anything!"

Could it be possible that they were unable to reach me? Had they given up after trying many times? Had they thought I was out of the country, as they often think because of my long absences from them? Sometimes my uncle asks me, when he sees me after a long absence, if I had gone on a trip somewhere during that time, and I say yes, so the visit won't deteriorate the way it usually does into making me feel guilty, which I always see as empty words my uncles use, empty words and nothing more, words that conceal irritation, or embarrassment, or shame, but not a sincere desire to see me. I don't remember them ever looking directly at me, into my eyes. And I certainly was never a "sight for sore eyes" to them. I never felt that at all. On the contrary, I'm just a teacher, a government employee, who collects his meager salary at the end of every month. I'm a person who can't be admired or depended on. And when it so happens that my name comes up in their conversations they always tell the story of what our old widowed neighbor asked me, the one who cleans houses to support herself because she has no one else to support her.

"How much do you make?"

I told her less than two hundred dollars (my monthly salary dropped even lower than that when the Lebanese lira plummeted during the war).

She said, "God will provide!"

My uncles tell this story and laugh heartily.

(If only the job were what bothered them about me, or if only the problem were my monthly salary!)

I had a sense of estrangement when I dialed the number to our house in Zgharta again. It felt as if I were dialing it for the first time in my life. I felt very uncomfortable and stressed; as if I were calling someone who was embarrassed to know me, or to be related to me.

I let the phone ring many times, but this time, unlike the previous time, I completely dispelled the notion that in my confusion I had dialed the number incorrectly. And I also dispelled the notion that no one could hear the phone ringing, because no matter where it might be placed in the house, it was impossible for no one to hear it from the parlor, which must have been full of women—my mother and female relatives and mourners—because according to our customs my father's body must be laid out on his bed in that room before the funeral procession and surrounded by the women night and day. And wasn't he the one who decided, when the house was being built, that the parlor should be big enough for occasions of joy and sadness?

I shouldn't take another tranquilizer, because it might put me to sleep. That's something I should avoid. Now I need to stay awake more than ever.

I shouldn't have given the newspaper back to my friend. I should have kept it so I could read it again.

I went to buy all the local papers that print that type of news. They all had the exact same phrase appearing in the daily police record:

```
TEL SQUARE, ZGHARTA, shortly after
noon Saturday, Hamad D. (age 60) was
murdered, a case of blood revenge.
```

Did that make the news—which I didn't doubt anyway—any more true? Why should I doubt it? It wasn't the kind of news that gets slipped into the press surreptitiously. Such a thing does not happen. The news of a revenge killing does not just slip into some newspaper or radio or TV broadcast. And what was more—and this is the most important thing—when I got back home I felt death had infected the things in my house. That's a feeling that only comes when the death is of a very close relative, like a father, or mother, or an uncle.

I made a mistake. I didn't leave the receiver off the hook so it would give a busy signal in case someone tried to call while I was out buying the newspapers. I felt a tremendous urge to call again, so I called and let the phone ring many, many times, my blood in a boil despite the tranquilizer I had taken, before a voice (finally!) I didn't recognize answered. The moment he picked up the phone and said hello I rushed to say, "This is Rashid. Is it true my father was murdered?"

"Two days ago," the voice answered. "My condolences. Such is life." He immediately added without pausing, "We moved the phone from the parlor," and then he hung up on me!

Was I dreaming, awake, or what?

Who was it that who answered the phone at our house, whom I didn't know, and who spoke using the pronoun "we"? "We moved the phone." I wanted to ask him his name, but he didn't give me a chance. And he hung up on me as though I were some parasite interfering in matters that didn't concern me! Did I take too many tranquilizers and now I'm confusing the real and the imaginary? Is that possible? Could one tranquilizer be too much? Or maybe I accidentally took two, but I doubt that completely because I am still conscious, and I am still able to weigh matters clearly and carefully, and I can still remember everything. In general and in particular.

Then I tried to call back several times but without success. The phone rang and rang and no one answered.

They disconnected it! Unbelievable!

That made me very nervous, just when what I needed most was to stay calm. But I did not give in to my desire to take another tranquilizer, especially since I figured that the person who hung up on me could well be one of those funeral directors they have in Zgharta these days. They're a very strange sort, showing up the moment they hear about a death to introduce themselves and the many necessary services they perform. Again I told myself there was no avoiding going to Zgharta right away. I had to go right away, without a moment's hesitation, no matter what dangers might be in store for me, for these dangers, serious as they truly might be, were not in reality extremely likely and could be averted with a good measure of caution. And furthermore, the dangers were far better than battling the fire of confusion, doubt, suspicion, and second-guessing. If I stayed at home, trying unsuccessfully to phone my family and find out from them what happened, and let them know I was coming, then I would remain prey to suspicions, and my coffee-shop friend's question would haunt me and torment me, filling me with anger toward my uncles, and toward my mother, too. And all that was uncalled for, especially if I could avoid it. I sat awhile gathering my strength and concentrating my thoughts in an attempt to determine what I should do in order to avoid doing anything I would come to regret. I also wondered to myself while in that state if it would be better to call Salwa and tell her what was going on before going to Zgharta. But I wavered between "yes" calling her and "no" not calling her. Calling her on this fateful occasion would be making a commitment to our relationship, amounting to a recognition by me of the depth and seriousness of the relationship, and an affirmation of its permanence, all of which would mean a clear and undeniable declaration by me that it was not just a fleeting relationship of convenience, based solely on our mutual desire for sexual relations and relaxing get-togethers, as I want it to be and to stay. And, calling her and telling her about the situation, and asking her to come would lead her without a doubt to tell her mother. That, in turn, would mean an affirmation from me to her mother of the "formality" of the relationship, which for all practical purposes could be construed by her mother as a "proposal"—indirectly, of course.

Salwa doesn't see our relationship the way I do. To her it is important, and that is why she tries deliberately and relentlessly to push it toward the public and the formal. She asks her mother, for instance, at least once a week, to cook a meal for me that she's good at preparing and that I like. And sometimes when the phone rings and she knows it's me calling she asks her mother to answer so I'll have to talk to her and greet her and announce my desire to talk to her daughter. "May I speak to Salwa please?" Or Salwa purposely says my name, loud and clear, *décontracté*, when she picks up the phone, to make her mother aware I'm calling and also to make me aware that our relationship is a household name. Not just between the two of us. Calling her at home under these circumstances would be a decisive blow in her struggle with her mother over whether I was attached to her or not. It would be a clear victory for Salwa, and she would say to her mother, quite upset, even before hanging up, "I'm going to Rashid's. His father was murdered!"

Oh God—that would be one more problem I don't need—her mother asking her where and how and who and when. Especially since Salwa would certainly spend the night with me if for some reason I was unable to leave for Zgharta tonight. She would never leave me alone at such a difficult time. And maybe she would stay up all night without sleeping so she could defend herself against her mother, for despite the fact that she can keep secrets, she can't always hide her emotions. If she slept, it would be next to me, in the same bed, and that would weaken her amid her mother's attacks, especially if she said to her, "Certainly you didn't sleep next to him with your clothes on!" But, if she didn't sleep, then she would be strong and stand up to her mother. "He stayed up all night, and I stayed up with him. He was miserable, waiting for a phone call. He tried to call…" She would not leave me, of that I am absolutely certain, and about that I am also (acknowledging the truth really is nothing to be ashamed of, nor is it a fault!) happy. I'd insist, of course, that she go home in the evening, so as not to burden myself with the responsibility of her staying over night, but she'd refuse, no doubt. And what's more, she'd be ready to do anything to help me deal with my situation. Every time her mother called, she'd complain, "I wish I could live alone! What a backward society!" (She complains that women are not free in our society.) Her mother would call her a lot, on her cell phone though (no way she would call my home phone) to ask her why she was so late, and what time she would be coming home.

"Shame! For your father's sake at least!" She'd resort to that excuse—Salwa's father—as she usually does whenever Salwa has a sound reason for being late. Then Salwa would be forced to give strong and sound excuses for staying, giving rise to her mother's nosiness and new questions being asked. One question would lead to another until they got to the crux of the matter, which is: Why didn't I attend my father's funeral? Salwa would be forced to bring her mother into it, that is if I do call her and ask her to come. (Or rather, she'd have her excuse.) No! I won't allow that. I won't allow anyone to be in such a position that compromises my extremely personal matters, especially not Salwa's mother, or even Salwa for that matter. Salwa doesn't know a lot of things about me, nothing beyond what she has seen and heard since we started dating. She learned long ago, from the beginning of the journey, that I don't like talking to her about my personal affairs—parents, childhood, personal relation-ships, marriage, divorce, etc. Just as she, too, for her part, is very frugal about telling me about her personal relationships. (Her relationships—plural?!) But actually she differs a great deal from me on this point. She always makes me feel she is prepared to exchange our personal histories. She's often setting up little traps for me to fall into, but I'm very careful. I've never felt I had anything to tell her, for one simple reason—opening up like that to one another is tantamount to an acknowledgment by both parties of the permanence of the relationship. An acknowledgment of its entirety—that is, of its completeness. It's not just a sexual relationship. And there's another essential reason I don't exchange personal things with her. What can I possibly tell her in exchange for the things she seems capable of telling me? Once she told me with complete candor and nonchalance—which made my head spin—that there was a time when she wanted to get pregnant by a man she was in love with—yet she was still with her husband. (She suffered from chronic anxiety when she was with her husband, always on the brink of a breakdown. Sometimes she took pills for it that her doctor prescribed. She said she met the man at some party, and told him her problems—all of them.) She said she didn't want a child from her husband, because she knew deep down that their marriage wouldn't last, despite the immense and sincere efforts she was exerting to make it work. She said that before her divorce she fell in love with a man and had a deep desire to get pregnant—an urgent need for it. She needed to feel like a complete woman, for through motherhood a woman is made complete. How often she had tried to persuade herself to get pregnant by her husband, and to persuade him, but whenever he would accept, deep down she would refuse, and so she would trick him and not let it happen. She felt he could not possibly be a good father, nor was he ready. Then when she met this other man and fell in love with him, and when he seemed so caring and respectful and considerate—before showing his true self and forcing her to abandon him—she wished she could have a child by him. She really wanted it. And she was prepared to claim it was her husband's in the event she was unable to get the divorce. Sometimes she felt she was capable of carrying out her plan by herself—keeping it a secret from both of them. It is pure happiness for a woman to get pregnant by a man she loves. But it's best, of course—especially for the child—for it to be with the father's knowledge.

I didn't say anything when she told me that, but she must have noticed the look of surprise or a little bit of shock on my face, despite my trying to keep my expression from changing—neutral, not expressing anything in particular. Then she added, "But as you can see, I didn't accomplish any of what I had hoped for during a very brief period of my married life. And the reason I didn't accomplish it is that I didn't want to, and that is an indication of something plain and clear." (Here, at this point in the conversation, she was quiet, to make me guess what the plain and clear thing was.

She meant that she used to dream sometimes, while under pressure—the pressure of the bad, miserable marriage—of total freedom. All that was nothing but a dream, which was the upshot of the pain she suffered because of her husband. But the dream never became a reality. She always maintained the highest moral standards, "in even the gloomiest of circumstances." She said that to reassure me that she was not the type to rush into things.

What she noticed in my expression, which she interpreted as shock, was not actually shock—it was merely an ember that flared up after the wind knocked off the ash. That is precisely what I was afraid of. I mean, I was afraid of talking about it with her, afraid of being obliged to reveal it, or dragged into it somehow—that is, to reveal the reasons behind the look on my face. And that was a strictly private, personal matter.

But now I need someone to exchange views with. Now, in these gloomy, decisive moments of my life. I need a friend, and not just anyone—maybe Salwa in particular.

Definitely Salwa. Salwa and no one else. No one listened more attentively to me when I discussed my problems, and no one was more patient or more ready to help—no—ready to make sacrifices for my sake. Salwa never tired of listening to me. Indeed, she enjoyed it. Sometimes, when I thought about the ways she hugged me and clung to me as though I were her sole salvation and having attained it never wanted to let go of it, or lose it, no matter what the cost, I told myself that she must really love me. I should be happy about that love. Rarely have I felt that my body is a precious treasure, which is how I feel with her. Indeed, rarely has any woman treated me with such rapture, with such patience, and with such caution—as though I were a one-of-a-kind gift she held in her hands and that could never be replaced.

Finally I decided to wait a little for her to call me, instead of rushing to call her, especially since she usually called me at that time of day—to ask me what I was going to have for lunch and show me how much she cared about me, though she never once thought of coming over to my house at noon to make lunch for me herself.

I decided after thinking long and hard about it that when she called I would tell her my father was seriously ill and would be transferred either today or tomorrow to one of the hospitals in Beirut for treatment. It could be any time. I felt this news would elicit the fewest questions. Then I would tell her the truth as soon as she got to my place. On the other hand, if she didn't call, then I would have to call her to tell her and ask her to come over, despite the consequences. It would be like backing down on my part, a clear and sudden indication of weakness. And it would create an imbalance in the equilibrium between us.

The phone rang while I was busy thinking about all that, so I rushed toward it. But before picking up the receiver I hesitated—in case the caller was a friend of mine who had read the news in the paper or some acquaintance calling to find out what hours condolence visitations in Beirut were being held. What would I say? What would I answer? But I couldn't not answer, because the call might be from her—from Salwa—and I really needed her now, deeply, and most likely it was Salwa, for this was the time she usually called. As I reached to pick up the phone, I regretted having taken the tranquilizer, because it kills my sex drive, but then I came to my senses and remembered that this was not the time for that. Then I came to my senses some more and thought, but why not? Surrendering to the tenderness of her hands and the warmth of her concern would be the greatest comfort of all. When she hugs me with her long arms and pulls me close to her, it is as though she is holding onto me for fear of falling off the roof of some tall building. I love that, and I admit it is endearing to me and takes away my worries and cares, and—why not—my sorrows, while I'm at it. Even if it happened now, it wouldn't be disrespectful to my father's memory, nor would it make me a *monstre*, and besides, I should just leave the matter to come in its own time—if it is going to come at all.

It was my uncle. My youngest uncle—my mother's friend Maryam's husband. I recognized his voice right away. The moment he heard me say hello he blurted, "God rest his soul. It happened Saturday, and yesterday, Sunday, he was buried. There's no need for you to come at all. It'd be much better to stay in Beirut, for your safety!" He didn't wait for me to respond or comment on what he had said, or to ask him anything. He simply hung up.

Unbelievable!

He didn't wait for anything from me—not a question, no grief, no shock, no anger, nothing at all. He spoke the words like a reprimand, as though he were speaking into a tape recorder and hung up when the recording was finished. What upset me the most was his thinking I stayed in Beirut out of concern for my own safety! In other words, that I stayed here despite my knowledge of the incident—meaning I knew!

Oh God!

It seems the virus of chaos is raging through the universe, attacking its logical defenses. Or something I cannot identify is eating up my individual ability to comprehend. Or maybe I'm being overly rational, burdening the intellect with more than it can handle.

True, what my uncle said was appropriate, and it's also true I kept silent while he did the talking, but I was listening in anticipation of more. I was waiting in particular for when he was going to say he was sending someone to get me and take me to Zgharta, because he knew better than anyone what the customs were and better than anyone what should be done, especially in such circumstances. Who knew better than he that the son of the victim was not to be left to come on his own, or that the son of the victim or any other relative who is so closely related should not be informed casually, not given the news like a tape recording. He should be told gradually, and be given a course of action to follow. He should be told, for example, that his father or his relative was in a car accident and was in critical condition, or tell him that he was shot but wasn't killed, and so on. The point is to tell him gradually, and then someone should be sent to pick him up and tell him the full, true story on the way.

My uncle knows that the "wounded one" could possibly hurt himself if he hears the news suddenly. He could hit his head or something without meaning to, or out of anger. He could do crazy things, because he feels directly responsible for his relative's murder, because he hadn't been able to protect him or hadn't cautioned him enough against the treachery of his enemies, or was ineffective at deterring them, or a thousand other reasons. Didn't my uncle remember our relative who hit his head against the wall when he left the shop to the sound of gunfire and saw a boy fleeing in terror, so he asked him what happened and the boy told him what he had seen and mentioned the name of the killer and the name of the victim as well, without thinking. Our relative hit his head against the wall just once when he heard the name of the victim—who was his brother—and fell to the ground unconscious. He was rushed to the hospital and came out weeks later, slowed both mentally and physically, and he is still like that to this day. Didn't my uncle remember that relative of ours, who was his neighbor and whom he saw every single day?

My uncle knew all of that. Indeed, no one knew better than he, so how could he hang up on me then, before the conversation had reached its conclusion? Like he was talking to a stranger. Or had I kept silent at a moment when he expected me to say something, and so he interpreted my silence to mean I didn't want to talk? But if I really did pause for a moment—and I don't deny it could have happened—then it would have been more likely that he would get worried about me. Who knows what effect a sudden blow of that sort might have? I could have paused because I was unable to speak from the shock. Then again, I don't remember pausing. In fact, I seem to remember that I was talking to him; I seem to remember the way I was following his words so carefully and the way I was reacting to them. Maybe he got the impression I was perfectly calm, completely in control of my emotions and reactions. That was true, because I was sedated from the tranquilizer I had taken shortly beforehand. But it was only one little pill, Ativan, 1 milligram. Had it been this calmness and self-control that gave him the impression I was cold and unconcerned, and so he got mad and hung up on me? But in reality I am not cold and unconcerned in the least. Maybe he was the one who was predisposed to seeing everything about me as cold and unconcerned.

But even supposing I made a mistake, a bereaved person should not be held accountable like a person under normal circumstances. A mistake made by a bereaved person is overlooked, and he or she is treated as if it never happened, or it's considered an indication of the depth of the bereavement. This is indeed the custom, so when did my uncle change his worldview and decide to speak to me in that curt manner—like a telegram? (I don't think anything about him—about my uncle—actually changed, rather, maybe the time had finally come for him to squeeze the pimple, so to speak, and drain the red hot anger from his heart, which had been there ever since his brother (my father) got married, and because of the circumstances surrounding my mother's pregnancy with me. In other words, since more than four decades ago, more than forty-three or forty-four years!)

And suddenly.

Suddenly, I felt myself preaching to the masses, saying, "Hey, people! Hey, all of you!"

But then I regained control and got myself back together, trying to make sure that everything was really happening. In practical terms, making sure required an extreme amount of concentration, the utmost concentration, because what was happening had never happened to anyone ever before. I have never heard of anything like it, despite having now reached the fifth decade of my life!

There is no other way but to go to Zgharta at once.

There is no other way to uncover this strange secret but to go myself, right away, before I am eaten up by misgivings and doubts, indeed before they do me in, especially since nothing is impossible when it comes to blood revenge. Nothing is out of the question. Revenge means murder, plain and simple. Not assassination, in that it's not a crime committed by an unknown assailant, or for unknown reasons, or both. On the contrary, vengeance must be brought into the open and discovered and confirmed, so everyone concerned can feel at ease. When the news of a vendetta killing reaches you, you're stupefied if you're a family member or relative or connected in some way or another. When the incident—which was essentially something you expected—happens, you're shocked more by *when* than by the fact of it. And if you're like me, "one foot on the fallow land and the other in the cultivated land," as the saying goes—in other words, I'm not exactly in that atmosphere and not exactly out of it either—then a multitude of conflicting emotions tugs you back and forth when you hear the news. Emotions like the desire to be violent and take revenge with your own hands, or the desire to be forgiving and call for peace and harmony, or to break the vicious cycle of revenge and give the rule of law a chance to prevail, or to just let matters run their course—and all that depends on who you are, what kind of person you are, or what your position or circumstances are and everything having to do with that.

Then things proceed as usual in matters of revenge, without any surprises or unexpected incidents—meaning with retaliation, or an attempt at retaliation, or with some final settlement, or a temporary settlement, or with pretending to forget about it until the proper time comes, or with just pretending to forget about it or something of that nature.

But for a blood-revenge incident to take place and then for things to proceed the way they had in this case was totally out of the ordinary.

I was calm, thanks to the tranquilizer I had taken and didn't regret taking one bit. Actually, I was prepared to go ahead and take sleeping pills instead of tranquilizers if I thought it was necessary. I was calm and my mind was clear and able to distinguish things in great detail. I could hear and listen with complete attention. My uncle should have realized that. How could he have allowed himself to interpret my behavior negatively? How could he hang up on me, in that abrupt manner, before the conversation was over? Before we had a chance to agree on a plan, like how I would get there especially, with whom and when and what was the safest route to take. And what's more, he didn't even give me a chance to find out who the murderer was. Who was it? Was he one of the customary "enemies"? Which one pulled the trigger? Or was it over some new disagreement I wasn't aware of? Or was it some kind of accident? Innumerable questions come to mind in such stressful moments. Why this insistence upon leaving me out of it? What did my uncle and his brothers stand to profit from that? What sort of profit were we talking about?

The one who called me on the phone was my youngest uncle. What existed between him and my mother was not love or affection exactly. In fact, he didn't like my mother one bit, nor did she like him. And that despite the truce they called after he married Maryam, my mother's closest friend and keeper of all her secrets and personal matters. For many long years there had been nothing between them except all-out public hatred of each other, and venomous messages carried back and forth between them by mediating tongues. The truth was they really didn't need mediators, since no one could understand the intentions of one toward the other better than they could, "in a flash," as they say. No one was as capable of instant communication as they were. A gesture, the presence or absence of one of them, a look, a sigh, an air of distraction, an attempt to say something, refraining from saying something, silence, and that sort of thing. When my mother would see him walking and comment on his gait, I would be surprised by the piercing intelligence that was revealed when she said, "Look at how he walks! Like he believes the earth is flat and he's afraid he'll fall off."

I call this kind of wit vicious.

Or when she would hear him analyzing or commenting on some bit of news he'd read in the newspaper, she would say, "He thinks he's the only Lebanese to learn to read and write since the days of the ancient Phoenicians!" (The Phoenicians being the inventors of the first alphabet.)

I always used to think to myself, whenever I heard these comments, that my mother was extremely intelligent and sharp-witted. If only she had had an opportunity to put her intelligence to use she would have accomplished wonders. These thoughts would lead me to think about the general situation in Lebanon, and the widespread notion that factions and religious sects fight with each other because they are ignorant of each other, and therefore the solution to the fighting is to get to know each other, because human nature is to hate what we don't know. Thinking about my mother would eventually lead me to say, "And why isn't it human nature to hate what we know oh-so-well?"

That same uncle of mine was the one who made a very malicious comment one time. I was saying to my cousins in his presence that I was the only one among all my relatives and friends who didn't have a brother or sister, and he said, "What for, so she could resemble her mother?" By that he meant that if I had a sister, she would resemble her mother—in other words, she would be venomous and of low moral character.

He said it in a very low voice you could barely hear, but I heard it with amazing clarity. It reverberated in my ear! I felt he realized how terrible it was to say, and that's why he lowered his voice to such an extent, so he could deny he'd said it if he had to.

No!

I will not fall into the trap.

Now that my father has been killed, my uncles will drag me and my mother to our demise if they can.

No. I will not be dragged into doing what my uncles want. I will not be dragged into carrying out their wishes. I will not avenge my father's death by killing his killer, or one of his killer's brothers or cousins. "No way," as they say in English. They cannot force me to do that! And what about my mother in all this? What is she doing now? She is keeping quiet for sure. Quiet! Mulling over her own worries all by herself.

(Her worries?)

I suddenly caught myself muttering these words in a very clear and audible voice. I was practically shouting.

So they didn't tell me about my father's murder in order to let me know that they don't hold me in very high esteem, and they don't grant me much importance. What was I to them but my mother's son, my mother whom they never accepted into the family for a single day, whom they did not consider one of their own. What was I but "educated." A literature professor at a university, who was useless in serious situations such as these. To put it bluntly, to them I was only partly a man—not a complete man.

But of what use was it to them for me not to attend my father's funeral? For me not to weep over his body and not receive condolences?

Did they think that by following this course of theirs they could startle me and jump start the blood through my veins? And thereby push me into doing what they wanted? Did they think they were capable of moving me from a distance, by remote control?

They didn't tell me because they wanted to put pressure on me and force me to avenge my father on my own. What wickedness! What barbaric wickedness! They want to say to me, "If you are really your father's son, our true blood relative, then go ahead!" They want to fill me with scorn in order to prove the contrary. Was this truly their goal? Were they plotting this to save themselves and their children in the first stage, so in case their plan failed to make me do it, then they would do it themselves? But they were wrong to begin with, if that's how they figured things out, for I will not avenge my father, nor do I want them to. That's old-fashioned, out of date—we're through with that kind of thing. I firmly believe that. And that, if they're trying to play me, is a firm and final decision that can't be tampered with. Period. As obvious as the sun. I am a contemporary man and I will not accept being anything less. Blood revenge is a thing of the past. Let my father and his brothers and his relatives and his friends and his enemies and his murderers… Let them all go to hell. How many times did I warn him about that vicious cycle from which there is no getting out or getting saved? And if they don't think I am a real man, then to hell with them. I don't need any declaration from them to be convinced of my manhood. And anyway, whether I'm convinced or not, that is my personal business. It pertains to me alone, and no one has the right to interfere in it. If being a man to them means behaving with their kind of bravado, or acting like a "tough guy," if that's what they call manliness, well then that's not my concern, because I don't possess that, nor do I want to. When they mock me with so much viciousness, their real aim is to say that I am not manly. I'm not daring, not bold, nor any other value having to do with blood revenge, which they treasure and value so highly. Manhood to them doesn't measure up (in importance) to manliness. Manliness is much more important, but the ideal is for both to come together in one person. Yes! As was the case with my father! Yes! My father was their perfect role model. What they all emulated. If they couldn't be like him, then they were awe-stricken before him, hands up in surrender to his superiority.

My father was nineteen when he began to take on those model characteristics of his. He made his debut as a "tough guy" by killing the husband of a woman he was intimately involved with. He always denied he did it, accusing her brother-in-law—her husband's brother—of killing his brother while drunk. People who were close to us, either as relatives or political allies, tended to believe his story, especially since the brother had tried to marry the girl himself when she was single. She didn't accept, and he pursued her a long time before finally giving up. Then afterward, he visited his brother's home frequently, especially after she had two sons. He was extremely affectionate toward them. My father would offer undeniable proof about the brother's guilt (and so on). He had seen him drinking *arak* only minutes before the accident. He'd greeted him, said "good evening" to him, and the brother tried to return the greeting but got tongue-tied. And there were witnesses (that is, others present). The storekeeper was questioned several times and swore to tell the truth, so it was the truth he told. And the truth, according to him, was that the brother bought a bottle of *arak* from him, in accordance with his usual habit of every two or three days. Yes! And he bought it in the evening—just before the accident occurred, maybe a half hour before. The brother wanted to kill his brother for asking him to stop coming to his house after they had a big falling-out over the inheritance and because the brother had his eye on the wife—the husband was often surprising his brother in various parts of the house he had no business being in, even if he was his brother. The wife was always very silent by nature, and especially in such predicaments, but despite that, she did acknowledge to him when he asked, that his brother did irritate her with his ogling, and the way he took too much liberty around their house bewildered her. In fact, my father participated in the funeral procession—proof of his innocence, for had he been the killer, how could he possibly do that? (My mother always smiled slyly whenever she heard that excuse, or whenever she told the story herself.) My mother saw him walking in the funeral procession with her own eyes, and that was before they got married. If she had known in time that he was the murderer, she never would have married him, not even if the whole world tried to force her to it. She would always say to her friend Maryam, "What an ignorant fool I was! If only I'd known about it before I got married, I could have saved myself from this hell." My mother found out after they got married that he was the murderer. She had detailed and reliable information no one could refute, and she also knew that the circumstances of the murder were not connected to the age-old enmity that existed between the two families, but rather to the relationship he had with the woman. That evening, the woman entered the bathroom—an outhouse, as was common in those days—to do something, wash clothes maybe, most likely to wash clothes in fact, because that was about the time the husband usually came home from work and she always let the dirty laundry pile up until that time—when her husband came home—in order to do all the wash at once. She was holding her infant son, who was less than a year old. My father saw her enter, and it seems it was still early in their relationship. He followed her inside and pulled the door shut behind him, though she had left it open as she usually did when she didn't go in to do something that required closing it—laundry, dishes, that kind of thing. The woman turned around and my father immediately wrapped his arms around her. She tried to push him off of her (my mother tells this story with uncanny precision, as though she's not relating some event but rather reading a scene she wrote herself about an event she herself made up, insisting on not leaving out a single detail, no matter how tiny). And while she tried to warn him of the incredible risk he was taking and how unbearably rash it was, and how she never wanted to see him again (my mother asserts that my father forced himself on the poor woman, who seemed to have made an innocent mistake the first time around, or did it without realizing what she was doing, and was subsequently taken advantage of by my father, who took her for all she was worth. "*Chantage*! That low-life!" my mother would say over and over to her friend Maryam.) And so while they went at it, the baby began to cry and his father came and opened the door on them and found them seemingly interlocked, my father holding up her dress and trying to enter her from behind, taking advantage of the fact that her hands and arms were occupied with holding the baby. The baby was bawling, terrified by not understanding what was going on. The husband charged at them without thinking, but before he was able to reach them, my father shot him dead. He ran off, believing no one saw him in the thickening darkness of the night. But my mother swears that many people did see him coming out of the outhouse right after the shots were fired, but no one wanted to get involved in a matter that might quickly evolve into a political, tribal situation, at a time when the skies were heavy with blood clouds in Zgharta and elsewhere in Lebanon—indeed in the entire region.

After that incident, the woman ran away to Beirut where she spent a life of complete anonymity and secrecy, having left behind her two small children. Her husband's brothers moved to another part of town because our house (I mean my grandfather's and father's family house) was very close to theirs, and the neighborhood, with so many of our relatives living in it, in effect belonged to us.

Whenever my mother reached the part about my father's attitude toward the woman after she ran away, her anger would double. My mother says my father didn't ask about her at all, after destroying her and turning her life into hell, as if he didn't even know her, never heard of her, never caused her any harm. He never once thought to ask about her, to find out if she needed anything or how she was getting along, or even at least to apologize. "That is an evil man!" my mother would repeat. "He enjoys seeing people suffer."

(I wonder now how my mother "mourns" my dead father, how she said her final goodbye. Is she sad? Does she feel sorry he's dead? Does his murder open up old wounds? Does she wish it had happened sooner, a long time ago, so she could have rebuilt her life as she wished? What is my mother thinking now, and how does she envision the next phase? Is she planning something?)

I saw the woman once in Beirut. That was the first and last time. My first year at the university. I went to the school where she worked just to see her, not for the reason I claimed—that I was looking for a teaching job. I wandered through the school, being careful not to meet up with anyone I knew and avoiding any situations that might require me to give my name, until finally I came upon her. I stood, taking a careful look at her without her knowing. She was just like all those Zgharta women I remember so well. Women from the fifties and sixties. She still wore the heavy black clothes in the same manner, nothing showing but her hands and face. I wanted to ask her why she was still wearing black when the mourning period had been over for so long, but speaking to her was not an easy task. I remember that I couldn't sleep that night, tossing and turning as I spoke with her. I would ask and she would answer. I would ask and she would answer until I became completely certain that my mother's story about my father killing her husband was correct. I asked her a lot about all those matters that had caused me so much anxiety my whole life. I asked her if my father had told her anything about his relationship with my mother before they got married, about how much he loved her and how attached to her he was. And I also asked her if my father ever mentioned Anwar—whom my mother was in love with at the time, and of whom my father was deathly jealous. I asked her in particular about the piece of paper he threw to my mother through the bathroom window, unsigned, in which he declared his love for her. All those things happened at that time. I asked her and insisted that she tell me what my father told her about the sexual relationship between my mother and Anwar. I really wished I had asked her if he ever said anything to her about his only night with my mother. That first and last night. I would have asked her very detailed and very specific questions—if he was still aroused after discovering what he discovered about my mother's virginity, or was he doubly aroused, and with what great force did he pour into her his anger and his desire, one single time, one first and last time.

But she didn't know anything at all about anything that happened after she left town. She was unable to help me with any of that, except to guess what his reaction might have been, even though she didn't really know him well—their relationship did not last long, nor was it very extensive during that short period. A few times was all. "He had been hunting for birds, and I was in the taxi on my way back from Tripoli, where I had done some shopping for my two children. It was dusk and just starting to get dark. He signaled for the taxi to stop and got in beside me in the back seat. He immediately overwhelmed me. I couldn't resist him. It was a moment of surrender. His hand roamed over my body wherever it pleased while I sat there shocked and completely taken by surprise, not consenting in my heart, and not resisting or refusing either. It was as though what was happening to me was happening to some other woman. But this other woman and I were sharing the same powerful pleasure at the very same moment."

Then he followed her into the outhouse the second time and she tried to fend him off, but he told her that she was the one who was making him linger. She was the one exposing herself and him along with her to the danger of someone barging in on them. If she had just gone along with him the moment he had entered, he would have been finished and out of there.

Two other times he drove her to Tripoli in a car he hired specifically for that purpose. He had seen her heading toward the taxi stand. He rushed over and insisted she get in. Scared someone might see her, she got in. On both occasions, on their way to Tripoli, he pulled over on a side road in the olive groves and forced her to let him do what he pleased.

She said—and this is precisely what my mother said, too—that the whole matter was merely a mistake on her part. Bad judgment. It was a moment of abandonment during which my father managed to rob her.

"Ignorance!" my mother said.

A little more than a year after the woman left town (they said she came out of the outhouse ululating, ran into her house, laid her baby down on the bed, and disappeared) my father married my mother. They spent their wedding night together, and shortly after that first night, a few days maybe, or a few weeks at the most (or maybe even before, who knows?) my father started seeing some other woman who had no children and who, like the first woman, was a few years older than he. Rumor had it that she could not have children because of her husband, not her. Whenever she was asked about it, she offered what many people considered a reasonable explanation. She would say, "God is the great giver!" Some saw in that an indication that the "problem" was with her husband. Three or four years had passed since their marriage when my father began seeing her intimately, and about two years later she gave birth to a baby girl. She didn't conceive any more children, which strengthened the notion that the baby was my father's. Which would make her about two years younger than I, not more. I didn't understand at first why my mother got so upset the day when that little girl came into our house with a group of kids. You would have thought a poisonous snake had just slithered between my mother's feet. She couldn't figure out how to get rid of her. I understood why later on. Once when I was twenty and the girl was eighteen or so, we began seeing each other. I liked her. She seemed beautiful and radiant and feminine. I used to meet her in secret. What encouraged me was that from the very first time we met, she relieved me of all suspicions concerning my father, by the way she treated me like any other person, but with a lot of affection. She was totally unaware of what was in my mind, or else she thought those were mere rumors and nothing more. Not based in fact. My mother found out that we went to the movies together in Tripoli, the next town over, despite all the precautions we took and despite our having adhered strictly to the plan we devised and carried out without a hitch. I went first to the taxi stand and made sure to get into a taxi with a driver who didn't know me and whom I knew nothing about except that he was a taxi driver on the Zgharta–Tripoli line, who only needed to pick up two more passengers before heading on his way. She and I had agreed that she should watch for the car and as soon as there were four passengers she should get in, making her the fifth. That would fill the taxi and the driver would then take off. That would cut down on the amount of time she would have to sit in the car waiting and exposing herself to being seen by someone while on her way to Tripoli without the escort of a family member or cousin. But unfortunately two passengers came in together. A man and his wife. So the car was full and the driver was ready to take off. I jumped up right away, claiming I had forgotten something, and we started all over again. This time it worked. When we got to Tripoli, our plan was to go way around the Zgharta taxi stand and then walk together to the cinema. We did that many times. Maybe three or four. One time, the taxi I got into by myself filled up with passengers right away and I couldn't make an excuse in time. The car sped off with me inside it, anger eating away at my insides. As soon as I reached Tripoli, I hopped into a taxi heading back to Zgharta. How my mother eventually found out, I don't know. It was a disaster! A veritable disaster! She nearly ate me alive! She could have killed me, she was so infuriated. She screamed and yelled at me so much the neighbors came.

She was yelling and saying things without mentioning the true reason for her anger, to the point that the neighbors who came and tried to figure out what the matter was couldn't understand anything except that I was a stubborn person who didn't take my future seriously. "He's a dimwit!" That is what she kept saying whenever she pretended to respond to their questions. The outcome of all my mother's frenzy was to forbid me from seeing that girl ever again. That girl, whose memory remained in my thoughts for a long, long time afterward. That girl, whom I dreamed of seeing again. My mother's volatile reaction caused all those old "suspicions" I once had to resurface. And once again I wondered about what people had said about the girl's father. I became certain that my mother was absolutely sure about the matter and that what she told Maryam was not just talk. In her mind, I had been having a relationship with my own sister. My thoughts eventually led me back to myself. Back to all the painful, worrisome, tortuous questions that I had just begun to put to rest. The unusual thing was that the girl never called me again after my mother blew up at me. She didn't even call to find out what happened, or to agree to stay apart from each other, as if by intuition she had gotten my mother's message, or as if word of the blow-up (my mother's blow-up) had somehow reached her, or as if her own mother had told her something. I don't know. In fact, I never even bumped into her on the street after that. She got married a few months later to an expatriate, emigrated to Australia with him, and never came back. I never heard anything about her again.

My mother never threatened me with my father, the way mothers threaten their children with their fathers when they misbehave. Except that one time! She told me she was going to tell my father, though she didn't say exactly what. All she said was, "I'll tell your father!" Threatening me with my father like that was a big shock to me. It was an event after which I expected to see more positive signs like it. Something that would lead to a renewal of their relationship. But I was wrong and had hoped to no avail.

My cousins on my father's side, to show how proud they were of their uncle (my father), sometimes used to say that I wasn't an only child. Meaning I had a sister. I remember once my uncle heard his son saying that, and he smacked him so hard he fell onto the ground with his lip bleeding. After that, it was never mentioned again. But this strong desire to cover up the matter and keep silent about it didn't mean that deep inside my uncles weren't proud of it. One time, my uncle fired a warning shot from his revolver for his brother (my father) when he saw the woman's husband coming home at an unusual time of the day. He knew his brother was over there. He always knew when his brother was there. A short while after the warning shot, my father stopped by and had a cup of coffee with him, without either one mentioning a word about it. Not a single word, as if the matter didn't really exist, so what was there to talk about?

My mother was aware of the intricacies of that secret agreement among the brothers, and she knew exactly why they were so proud of their brother. It infuriated her to no end. She often said to me on such occasions that my uncles made her feel like vomiting. She didn't want me to be like them, but then she would correct herself and add, "But you are one of them!" I would fall silent, unable to speak. I could not tell her that in my heart I did not love my uncles because they despised me. I felt that this attitude of mine toward them was against my father, so I hid it deep in my heart.

My uncles had their reasons for loving their brother and regarding him as a role model. That was their business, which I never once thought to bring up with them, but for them to force their values on me, to make me emulate them in order to become "my father's son" in their eyes—that I did not accept. In the first place, I don't believe in those values, nor do I consider people who hold them worthy of esteem or respect. So how could I accept them as men with qualities and characteristics I should constantly emulate?

No! No way!

I am definitely not like my father. I didn't inherit the two characteristics. There weren't any stories going around about how I fathered children from married women who used me for their own purposes to undermine their husbands. And I didn't murder anyone or avenge anyone and I didn't flaunt my brazenness or attack anyone. And I didn't marry a woman I would sleep with only one time— the first and the last—on my wedding night. Because I discovered she was not a virgin and figured out it was Anwar, whom I hated, who beat me to it, to that place I dreamed would be mine and mine alone, that no one would beat me to, or follow me to, and so I didn't dare talk about it openly, about why I treated her so harshly my whole life after having pursued her so intently years before and tricked her into marrying me, and so I left her in my house, for fear of some sort of scandal, rather for fear that some other man would get to that place after me, but never would I come near her ever again after that first time on our wedding night! The night she conceived a son who lived part of his life (only part of it?) within the nightmare of not being his father's biological son, a son who lived his whole life as an estranged fruit, shunned by the branch that bore it.

I don't think my uncles are ignorant enough to expect me to behave like my father. I have nothing at all in common with my father, except for what I inherited from him. No one knows that better than my uncles, so why are they betting on me?

I will not avenge him!

And if they were expecting me to avenge him, they were making an unbelievably huge mistake. Was it even possible they could make such an immeasurable mistake?

Were they that oblivious to me? Were they blind? I ask and wonder out of curiosity and nothing more—the curiosity of someone who knows the answer. I know them as well as they know me, perhaps even better, much better. Oh, for certain much better. My uncles never loved me, not for a single day. I never felt they treated me with the kind of affection due a nephew.

I will not take revenge. And that's final!

What I will do to compensate for him as my father is take his murderer to court. I will take his murderer to court. That is my father's right and my obligation. For despite everything, he was my father, and I his son. True he was not the father I wished him to be, but if he had been like other fathers, he would have been as proud as can be for having educated me to the level of a university professor. And he could have been proud also for having forbidden me from carrying guns and getting involved with guns despite the situation and the problems we were having that required keeping weapons and becoming as used to them as a kitchen knife, or a plate, or a spoon.

He educated me. I pursued my studies thanks to him. True, he didn't keep close track of me, but my staying in school was surely his wish, as was my attending university. He was prepared, no doubt about it, to sacrifice everything for that purpose. From the day I started school he began proclaiming his wish for me to learn French, the most prevalent foreign language in the country at that time (it still had not been very long since France had withdrawn its mandate from Lebanon). Without French, as he used to say, a person cannot get anywhere. He bought me an Arabic–French dictionary. I still have it. He bought it of his own volition, before I really even had any need for it. That gesture was a complete surprise to me, and it left an impression on me I'll never forget. As he handed it to me he said, "Don't let go of it!"

I was tongue-tied, not knowing how to respond. What did it mean, that order, that advice—not to let go of it? It was like a grenade in my hands ready to explode at any moment. I really did not understand the necessity for it. Yet when my father gave it to me he was absolutely certain of what he was doing—which was what made me think he knew what he was saying and that there was no doubt I should make the constant effort to be forever poring over it and memorizing the information it contained and gazing at the illustrations to know what they signified. The next day at school I told my teacher about my father's wish and confided to him about my anxieties and fears. He said that the dictionary was merely a resource to be referred to when necessary, that was all. So I immediately repeated that to my father, who said, "Of course. It is to be your life-long companion."

And my father strictly forbade me from using guns— though I knew exactly where in the house he kept them hidden. He always used to ask me to bring them to him for maintenance. He would clean them and sun dry them and oil them routinely, and then tell me, "Put them back where they belong and forget they are there!"

Truly my father could take pride in all that, but he was a quiet father, who especially didn't express emotion. He was not good at that. But I didn't need him to express his feelings in order to understand them. I understood them. Who was he, after all, but my father, and who was I but the offspring of his loins, his own flesh and blood.

(That's why it was natural to a certain extent for me to feel that strange feeling toward the objects in my house when I went home after hearing the news of his murder. That strange feeling that the things had somehow contracted the contagion of his death. And it was also natural for that feeling to make me say deep down inside, Yes! For certain it was my father who died! At the time I wanted to reply to my friend's question that yes, I was absolutely certain that the man who was murdered was my father and no one else. The feeling was both strange and comforting at the same time, which is a huge paradox for sure, but life's path is not always easy and straight.)

I'll raise a case against the killer. That's my father's right and my obligation. And I will not drop the charges in return for some monetary compensation offered for reconciliation between the two families, no matter how much I am pressured. I'll declare before everyone that I am not responsible for what my uncles or cousins might try to do, or for what someone else might try to do at their beckoning. They are responsible for themselves. That way I could kill two birds with one stone, and follow my conscience as both a son and a citizen. The time has finally come to allow the law to prevail. That is certainly more humane than customs that have come to us from prehistoric times.

I am a man who feels a strong sense of civic duty.

I am a man with a strong sense of humanity.

I'm one of those people who, if they heard that the sun's temperature was decreasing, they would conserve hot water. They would do their part to preserve the earth's heat as much as possible, in case the problem persisted a long time, thus allowing the human race a chance to find a way to avert disaster. So how could I take revenge for my father, and against whom? Could I possibly conceal a revolver at my waist and lurk in some corner, waiting for the murderer to pass by so I could waylay him, pull out my revolver and fire at him once, twice, three times? And possibly not even shoot the real murderer (because he would usually be extremely cautious) but some relative of his instead? Could I possibly do that? Have we not yet stepped into the age of the modern nation, the nation of laws? Is it right for me, or anyone else, to take the law into my own hands in this twenty-first century?

I don't hide the fact that I'm spouting all this civilized talk despite the raging emotions afflicting me, that the hand that killed my father was a cruel and horrid one. That hand—yes that hand destroyed my father, from whose loins I sprang into this world—whose flesh and blood I am! I despise his killer and do not forgive him at all for what he did. No, more than that, I sincerely hope I never come in contact with him, especially not now, because I cannot guarantee I will behave the way someone like me should behave. My blood might boil over, causing me to pounce on him and murder him. Yes, my blood might boil over. Boil over! I did after all come from my father, like anything comes from some other thing, like the branch comes from the tree trunk, like the tree comes from the earth. What would happen if he could witness the fact that now I will not avenge him. He would be very angry, and the world would darken around him, and he would wish he were alive, if only for one minute, just to punish me.

How would my father, my dad, punish me, when as far back as I can remember he never hit me once. We weren't "friends" or anything, as is the fashion these days— for dads and sons to "be friends" and speak openly about all kinds of issues. He didn't pay close attention to me, but he was not stern with me, either, or violent. Any feelings I had concerning sternness or violence came as a result of that unnerving silence that stood forever between us like a high, thick wall.

I honestly don't know what his reaction would be to my refusing to avenge his blood. Actually, I wonder if he might have expected that from me. It was he, after all, who pushed me to become educated and forbade me from using guns.

Oh God!

This is all I need to finish me off, to do me in completely—for my father to be killed "for reasons of blood revenge" as it was stated in the newspaper.

Indeed, for the news to reach me two entire days after his murder, after his funeral and burial!

Why don't you call me, Salwa? Why so late this time? Why aren't you dying to see me today? Why resist calling me today of all days? Why did you choose today of all days not to play this game you never stop playing? If only you could know the key to me today to make me tell you, to make me share my past with you in return for your stories! My story will amaze you, Salwa. My past will shock you. And you'll find out that your suffering was nothing compared to what I've been through.

Or is it that you read the news in the paper and were surprised to know I belong to a social milieu that still values blood-revenge traditions, and now you've withdrawn suddenly from my life without any indication or warning.

Salwa reads the newspaper every day. It's a habit of hers. And she reads nearly all of it, starting with the inside sections—the local news and miscellaneous news—then she goes back and reads the front page and major headlines.

Salwa said to me once, "You northerners are still living in the Jahiliyya. You still haven't been enlightened by Islam! Or Christianity for that matter." And I remember that I was very accommodating and joked that northerners were the ancestors of man, not apes like Darwin said. She really liked that. She hugged me close to her, rewarding me for my sarcastic spirit. Salwa, like her mother, doesn't generally like northerners, and it pleases her for me to talk about them like I don't care. She really likes it when I mention their shortcomings or anything she might consider negative. The thing her mother hates about me most of all is the fact that I'm from the north.

When I told her that northerners were the "first humans," she asked, hoping for more derogatory remarks, "And what did they originate from?"

"Goats!" I exclaimed.

Northerners descended from goats! That's why they lived so high up in the mountains—not to escape oppression, as they claim. Only goats are capable of living in those rugged mountains.

Salwa listened to me say those words as if through her mother's ears. She listened so closely, memorizing every word, in order to pass it on to her mother without leaving out a single detail. She really wanted her mother to accept me wholeheartedly. She dreamed of it, in fact. That would put her at ease, and she also thought it would allow her more freedom in her relationship with me.

Salwa loved hearing me say that. She saw it as my way of distancing myself from the people of the north and consequently bringing myself closer to her and where she was, still fixed in place at home with her parents and relatives.

Now that she has read about the incident in the newspaper, which undoubtedly erased that distance that endears me to her, well, she must have "slammed on the brakes" suddenly and involuntarily. She stopped calling me without making a conscious decision to do so. She probably said to her herself, "What do I want with those people? What do I want with revenge and all its worries and troubles! I have nothing in common with that far off world. Let me keep away from it. I cannot live in constant fear for my husband and my children, fear they might be murdered, and fear they might be obliged to commit murder!"

Salwa has every right not to like this world, and not to become a part of it. She has every right not to dress in black most of her life or spend her whole life or a big part of it anyway waiting for her husband to get out of jail, or to come home when he can, or when it's safe. She shouldn't have to rush outside to ask everyone about the gunshots she just heard being fired, who shot them and at whom. She has the full right to refuse to have her world divided into three zones—a safe zone, a hostile zone, and a zone in which she must be always on her guard—she being the one who loves life, loves moving from place to place, taking trips, on foot or by car, by herself if she can't find a companion, she who surprises me from time to time by saying things like, "I was in Tyre today," or "I was in Tripoli." And if I ask her, "Why?" or "What were you doing there?" she responds with "I just felt like it." One time she told me she got stuck in Dahr el-Bayda on her way back from the Bekaa because there was a bad snowstorm and the roads were closed. She said that the snow was almost as high as the car window, and that she was not afraid. After all, she never felt afraid anymore since getting a cell phone. I asked her, "Why didn't you call me when you were stranded there?" She said, "Why should I call you when you never worry about me?" Then she said, "If you had gotten stuck, would it have occurred to you to call me?"

Could Salwa possibly decide to cut off our relationship without hearing me out? Without knowing from me what happened and my opinion about it? Am I now the one who is being threatened with abandonment by Salwa? Is that why she hasn't called? If that's really the reason she hasn't called, then it's a closed case. I mean, our relationship is over. I'm ending it right now. Which means I must face this situation on my own, without depending on anyone, because no one is going to come to my rescue as I had expected. What I must do immediately is go to Zgharta. There is no way out of doing that. Every moment spent in hesitation is just putting off the inevitable. I must go by taxi, because I won't be able to drive myself. I won't be able to focus and concentrate. Too bad, because I really love my car, which I haven't owned for very long. Barely two months. It's a 1993 Mercedes 300 Full Option. I paid twenty thousand dollars for it. I put ten thousand down and borrowed the rest. If only I could find someone to come along with me and drive my car. Then I'd be able to drive it back, because on the way back I will have had a chance to calm down and relax a bit. At any rate, it's safe from being stolen or hit if I leave it here, because I pay a monthly fee to keep it in a lot that's guarded day and night.

Thinking about such matters at a time like this is nothing to be ashamed of. Life is harsh, and money is hard to earn. And in practice I generally don't think about these matters. They're simply fleeting notions that cross my mind uninvited. I'm fully prepared, actually, to sacrifice that car and everything else I own, if it would make any difference. I won't be able to drive my car myself. Of that I am completely certain. Nor is there a friend I can call on to accompany me and drive. That's not something you can ask just any friend to do. It's dangerous, even if only slightly. And it's pushing someone into something that is not polite at all to push someone into, especially someone who is not involved in it somehow.

I must go by taxi, no matter how much it costs. There's no question about that. It wouldn't make sense to take a "service" taxi or the bus, thereby exposing myself between stops to the possibility of running into some people from the village who know about the matter and have them ask me about it and offer condolences or show their shock or, or... No!

I'll take a taxi! Period.

And besides, a taxi is much faster than other means, especially at night when there are fewer passengers and there's a long wait for a "service" or bus to fill up and take off.

I must go right away, because staying here will not do me any good. Here I am vulnerable to all kinds of strange ideas that pounce on me and burn my insides. But how can I go to Zgharta before contacting someone there and consulting with him? How can I go without knowing what awaits me, what earth-shattering event?

Oh God! I'm still stuck here unable to take initiative! What if I were to contact some of my friends there—those old friends who didn't even contact me to break the news or to console me at the very least. Why? That makes the whole situation even more bizarre.

It really is a big deal! And I'm not wrong about this. It's even bigger than I ever imagined. Much bigger.

What does it all mean?

My father was killed and no one contacted me, including my own relatives, or any of my old friends, my childhood friends, my companions on muddy roads, in narrow alleys, and between damp cement walls. No one contacted me about this momentous event, so what does that mean? What is going on? My head is spinning. My head is boiling over. What's going on? Now I wish I hadn't taken that tranquilizer when I heard the news. I should have saved it for now, because my head is boiling over even more than before. Not one word from anyone, and it's been three whole days since the incident. And what an incident. The murder of my father. My father was murdered! He did not die a natural death at a ripe old age. Did my uncles, or one of my uncles, kill him, causing some kind of family embarrassment and that's why people kept to the themselves and failed to offer the obligatory condolences? Did this crime shake up the very foundations of their social order, go beyond what is customary in these matters, causing them to be bewildered and unsure of what to do and what not to do? Did this strange new situation prevent them from carrying out their traditional mourning practices?

All the newspapers said that the murder took place at Tel Square, in broad daylight, at 12 o'clock noon, and that it was a matter of blood revenge. But what does it matter what the newspapers say, based on police reports. No actual reporters were on the scene, and there was nothing added to the police account from any source.

And really, what do such accounts have to do with what actually takes place on the ground? No one is willing to divulge what he sees or hears. Rarely does a witness speak up in blood-revenge cases. And if one does, it is with the knowledge of and in agreement with the three concerned parties. I mean by that the two opposing parties and the third one involved in settling the matter. Fear, sense of futility, shame, and not wanting to get involved, all these prevent people from coming forth as witnesses.

Yes! Yes, I said *shame*.

So many people do not want their dirty laundry hanging out on the rooftop for all the world to see, relatives and strangers alike. It's much better to hide it.

And so here I am, still right here where I started from, not having made one step of progress. My brain, on the other hand, is speeding out of control, going in all directions at the same time.

My brain is spinning around a million times a second. But how can a brain spin around? That's just talk. I need to calm down. I was about to say I need another tranquilizer.

Could my uncles have been the killers and conspirators? But why? I can't see any reason why they would. They loved and respected him very much. He was their elder brother and everything that title carries with it in our culture. They walked in his footsteps, following and obeying his every step. They would seek his advice on every issue, big or small, never making a move without his blessing. He truly was what you call the "head honcho." He was the "chief of the tribe," even before their father (my grandfather) died. They knew every detail of my father's matters and affairs, including the private and romantic ones. And they had their opinions concerning his affairs, too, and opinions about how he should behave with my mother, both when he was in love with her before they got married and after they got married, too. He might not have told them exactly what he wrote on that note he asked his youngest brother to toss to my mother while she was bathing at home in her bathroom. But they did know the reason behind the big fight between them and Anwar and Anwar's relatives out in the schoolyard. They knew the reason, if not all the details. They knew their brother was in love with her, even if he hadn't said so. And they knew there was something between her and Anwar, and that she was leaning toward Anwar, not their brother. They also knew how angry this made their brother. They figured that out right away, right from the start. And they told him what they were thinking without hesitation and with absolute frankness. In fact, when the couple announced their plans to be married, they told him she was not fit to be his wife and the mother of his children. Because, they said, she was not the right type for a life like his. "She's not one of us!" they said. "Yes, she's beautiful and educated, but she's not one of us!" But he was infatuated with her and incapable of making such calculations. His calculations were not like his brothers'.

He told his youngest brother to toss the note through the bathroom window, without telling him what the note said. My mother was bathing.

He wrote just one line: *Wear your yellow dress to school tomorrow.*

He didn't sign the note or leave any indication it was from him. My father assumed my mother would know immediately who the sender was. He was certain she was aware of his affections, especially since he hinted about his feelings several times. He didn't let a single occasion pass without trying to convince her how very useful he was to her, how very necessary. At the same time, he knew a lot about her feelings for Anwar and her interest in his affairs. And about her relationship with him, too, that had begun to develop and take tangible form.

He knew everything that transpired between my mother and Anwar. No gesture, no matter how silly or meaningless, went unnoticed by him. By some deep and penetrating sense, he perceived everything that went on between them.

My father wrote that note because he sensed that the relationship between my mother and Anwar was about to take tangible form. Until that point it had been limited to glances and admiration, to being in the same place at the same time, to being quietly and vaguely responsive and sensitive to each other's desires, like things are between two people on the verge of revealing their feelings. With his note, therefore, my father had wanted to turn the tables and disrupt the situation before it had a chance to become a reality. He waited for her reaction, but it didn't come! (My mother thought the note was from Anwar, not him. She insisted on that, and still does.)

Shortly after the note was sent, my father's and Anwar's eyes met. It happened at school, during a moment when heaven abandoned the human race. The next thing anyone knew the two of them were tangled in a brawl, swinging their fists at each other like archenemies. They were aiming directly at each other's most vulnerable spots. The head, the balls, the gut. Then a team rallied behind each one. No one who spoke about the incident could say exactly what had started it. There hadn't been any storm clouds in the village sky at the time, no lightning in the atmosphere. There was not any animosity between the families that might have given fair warning about what happened (between the two boys). No one had seen them arguing before the fight. They looked at each other and the fight instantaneously sparked on eye contact. My father wanted to fight Anwar in order to nullify Anwar's relationship with my mother. And Anwar did not refuse to fight, emboldened as he was by my mother's affections for him, which pleased him a great deal for sure. (Had the incident with the note gotten him excited? Had he said he was the sender when he saw how much she wanted that to be the case?) My father was well aware of the details of that relationship, which was still in its infancy and had not yet come fully into existence. He could imagine what might happen if he didn't put a stop to it right away. What irritated him most of all was that he was sure Anwar didn't really love her and was only going to "play around with her." All Anwar wanted was to get physical with her. (Only to the extent that customs in those days would allow. He never dreamed of going further than that! Of going as far as my mother dreamed!) Then after he did with her what he pleased, or what he could, he would dump her and leave her to wallow in disappointment and regret and jealousy, and all those emotions. Whereas my father, on the contrary, truly loved her and wanted to marry her as soon as possible.

My uncles joined the battle with all the enthusiasm and desire for victory brothers can muster. Each blow was intended to be decisive. And when the police arrived after the principal called and requested intervention, my uncles put their youngest brother out in front so that if the police had to arrest any of the boys who were fighting, they would arrest him, a minor. That was the least they could do for their brother.

They loved him and he reciprocated their love and loyalty. When my youngest uncle got married, my father helped him build his house. He paid for more than half the expenses. He felt responsible for his brothers' standard of living, and never allowed any of them to be without any necessity.

This remained the case, even through their most difficult times, which is why it would be impossible for such brothers to fight with each other. Certainly they could never kill each other.

No. No way!?

If there was one person my uncles wanted to kill, it was my mother. They hated her, despised her. There is no question they wanted her dead. To them she was like a viper slithering among them, under their arms and in their laps. Day and night they dreamed of getting rid of her. When I think about it, I'm amazed they haven't gotten rid of her yet somehow or other. In our town, as is the case all over the Bekaa region, such a thing is not unheard of, for a man to kill his wife and no one ask anything about it. A woman might get shot in the leg during the war, for example, and her husband would take her in his car to the hospital, insisting on going alone, and then on the way he might pull out his revolver and shoot her in the head at close range, and she would arrive at the hospital dead. There were others whose wives were shot by a stray bullet by mistake while at home at the usual time, and when the husband heard her scream, he went and shot her with his own gun, one shot, in some vital spot, and then started crying out to neighbors and relatives for help.

It is strange how no one has ever attempted to get to my mother. Indeed, no one has ever dared speak an ugly or improper word to her. Everything that has transpired between her and her adversaries has passed with utmost silence.

Perhaps what agonized my mother most of all were my father's extremely contradictory feelings toward her and the absence of one strong singular emotion capable of eradicating the others. My mother, however, did not possess multiple and contradictory feelings toward him. She had one and only one feeling for him, and that was hatred. She hated him. But she was afraid of him, and her fear paralyzed her will (not her desire) to run away. "If only I could run away!" she always repeated to Maryam, entrusted keeper of all her secrets. "But where would I go?" she would add. She was very afraid of him and convinced he could find her no matter where she ran. She was scared to cross him because she knew it would cost her dearly. "Remember?" she would say to Maryam. "Remember how he confined me to the house the first few days of our marriage, and forbid me from going out for an entire week? He locked the door and all the windows!"

Maryam would always ask my mother how she managed with my father on their wedding night, and my mother always insisted she didn't do anything at all. There is no doubt my mother was being truthful. She was known for her stubbornness. Maryam always liked to ask that question, which aroused my mother's desire to talk. How did he not discover anything? How? And my mother would answer, "Do you really believe that? Do you believe he didn't discover anything?" And my mother would start again to tell the story of her first night with him. The way my mother told the story of her wedding night, and the way Maryam listened to it and her reaction to every single detail, was a kind of ritual they practiced together. Everything was *previsable* from beginning to end. They would continue on and on until the part where they were cut off. And they were always surprised and amazed at the same part. As if it were happening for the first time. They would get all worked up over the same response and fall silent at the same part that was difficult to respond to, and so on.

After my father forced her, in that vengeful manner, to take her clothes off, my mother didn't make a sound. She just let him do what he wanted, surrendering to his will and his growing desire. She made no sound except to scream whenever the pain became too much to bear. Even then she tried to conceal her cries, because everything that was happening to her now and everything that might happen to her in the future, she was responsible for. She had no choice but to bear the consequences of the decision she had made for herself and which no one forced her to make. She surrendered to her fate, as if by some irrefutable volition willing her to do so. As for him, the more she screamed and the colder and more unyielding her body became, the more he wanted to hurt her. And despite being aroused, he noticed, in a big way, her coldness and refusal. Then, after that—not long at all after the whole encounter began, that is—he lunged into her only to discover how unexpectedly easy it was. And so he stopped for a second, frozen, before resuming in a blind frenzy, as if he had suddenly gone crazy and wanted only to hurt her, to tear her apart, to mutilate her.

"He was getting back at me. Yes. The only thing preventing him from killing me was wanting revenge on me so badly. He wanted revenge, and he knew you can't take revenge on someone who's already dead."

Next my mother would tell Maryam how the moment she entered the bedroom he asked her to lie on the bed and take off her clothes, just like that, one sentence. She stood there, looking warily and timidly about the room and at the bed, which was ready and waiting. At first she hesitated, and then she sat on the edge of the bed and said in a barely audible voice, "Be gentle."

He interrupted her hastily and said, "I told you to lie down and take off your clothes." Then he walked over and turned off the lamp, leaving the room illuminated by the light from the street that came in through the sheer curtains covering the window. When he saw her still sitting there on the edge of the bed, he approached her and slapped her on the face. Once, twice, and then he hit her over the head. Then he bent down tensely, lifted her two legs off the floor and threw her onto the bed so her whole body was stretched out on top of it. Then he said, "For the last time, take off your clothes!" So she took off her clothes, hardly believing what he was doing to her. It was as though he were carrying out a plan he had prepared ahead of time. She didn't want to take her clothes off, but she was in no position to say no.

"Of course not!" Maryam would say when my mother reached this part of the story. "You did not have the right to say no to him. You became his wife of your own will. If he'd let you behave as you pleased, you never would have let him come near you!"

My mother was in trouble. She didn't know what to do, or how she should act. So she submitted to his orders, hoping that perhaps he would be less volatile after a little while and she could work things out in her own way. She undressed down to her underwear, of course. "After all, this was my very first time. True, I sometimes met Anwar and we would embrace" (at this point in the story of her marriage my mother would sigh and her cheeks would turn red). "I obeyed Anwar without any resistance. I let his hand wander about and invade my entire body, to push aside whatever bit of clothing got in its way. And he would take my hand and kiss it and find great physical pleasure in that, as if he were being blessed by it. Then he would put my hand where earlier I had said no. But after a while I didn't resist, as it made him very happy. He cried out in a way that frightened me at first. Later it pleased me, but I was worried someone passing by the photographer's studio where we always met would hear him.

"No—my encounter with Anwar was nothing like this one. Not only was Anwar completely different from this guy (my father, that is) but from all the other boys in town. Did I show you the pictures he took of me?"

"Of course!" Maryam would reply while my mother headed off to the bedroom to get a wooden box full of things she kept hidden in the closet. She would come back with it and show the pictures to Maryam, except for two pictures that she only very rarely showed her, because those were hidden away in a place that was difficult to get to quickly. (Those two pictures are at my house now. I got them many years ago when I happened to find my mother's passport, with a visa for Egypt stamped by the Egyptian embassy in Beirut.)

"But that man!" my mother would say, continuing the story of her wedding night. "That man!" (And she meant my father.) "Turned out to be very strange, even though I had known him a long time. He's a relative. The enemy within!"

Then my father reached for her bra and snapped the strap so hard it hurt her. So she begged him to slow down. ("Imagine, Maryam, there I was begging him, the same man who never skipped a single day trying to get me to marry him!") Then she took off all her clothes, slipped under the covers and pulled them all the way up to her neck. She was trembling. She turned her back to him.

"Aw. She's shy!"

My mother has never forgotten those words he shot at her like a poison dart, and she never will as long as she has a pulse in her veins. Never before had she felt so insulted and so full of anger and hatred as in that moment. Every time she recalls that moment her blood boils and gushes through her body, nearly bursting her veins. My father shot those words, that "poison dart" as she called it, even though he had yet to confirm his suspicions concerning her having already lost her virginity. Rather, he had said it rashly, out of anger at the way she pretended to be shy and innocent, knowing that he knew all about her many "dubious" meetings with Anwar. He was incapable of imagining that she could be so happy and relaxed with Anwar and go freely to meet him and yet be so tight and cautious and shy and forced with him. As if a woman were free to make use of her body to please whichever man she happened to be with, even if that man was her own lawfully wedded husband!

At this point my mother felt she had committed the biggest mistake of her life. "I deserved it!" But it was impossible now to turn back, even if it had only been a matter of hours since her wretched decision to marry my father. "True it was my decision and I do not hold any one else responsible for it. But he" (my father that is) "was not entirely innocent. He came to me at exactly the decisive moment! As if he knew the time was just right."

But despite everything, my mother never considered getting back at him personally, or ruining his life. She always blamed herself instead. If she hadn't accepted his proposal of her own free will, he never could have forced her; no one could have forced her. Sometimes when she thought about revenge, she would say that she should take revenge against herself and no one else. Sometimes she would say things in front of me like, "I'd be better off dead and buried!" So now had everything changed after all these years that have led me to live permanently in Beirut only rarely visiting my mother? Maybe once a year, twice on occasion. Had everything changed now to the point that she couldn't take it anymore? Had she actually reached the point of desiring to take revenge against him, indeed the point of deciding to actually do it?

Could that be?

But the newspapers said the murder took place at noon, in Tel Square, which is the main square in town! But what would the papers know? What do the papers ever know? The world is in one place and the papers are somewhere else, especially when it comes to our part of the world.

Could it have been my mother who killed him, with her own hands? With the revolver he always kept under his mattress near his head, or maybe with some poison she sprinkled on his food? Or maybe she switched the pill he takes once a day to lower his cholesterol. How could my mother have killed him? Did she hit him over the head with a hammer while he was sleeping? My father used to snore a lot, and my mother always complained to Maryam (not to him!) and confided that sometimes she spent the whole night unable to sleep because of it. Had he been snoring so loudly that night that she lost control of her anger, grabbed something heavy, made of iron or stone or whatever would serve the purpose, and hit him over the head with it as he slept? My mother didn't dare move her mattress into another room because she didn't want to rouse his anger (and now I would say his suspicions, at least that was the case for a period of time).

"He forbid me from my own life," she would say. And she would protest this tyranny. For a person to pay such a high price for a mistake he or she made in an absent-minded moment while still so young and ignorant of the world, truly was tyranny.

Was she the one behind this wall of hellish silence that was built up around me to prevent me from knowing about my father's murder at the appropriate time? Did my uncles say something like, "Our brother has been murdered and now all that is left is this snake and her son. So what do we care about them!"

Did my uncles say, "What do we care about that snake and her son who is not really our son (one of ours), not our brother's son!" They had their doubts about whether their brother, my father, was really my father. They probably believed I was not his son, because they were privy to everything that went on even in private. They were privy to what happened between my mother and my father on their wedding night, and they were privy to what never happened again after that night for the rest of his life, right up until his murder.

"What do we care about that snake and her son?" my uncles said and took off, each one to his own house, after performing the obligatory duties. Did the war of poisonous silence between them finally break out? But if this supposition was correct—if she killed him, or if she masterminded it—they would kill her. It would be easy for them, too. All they would have to do is go to her house at night, since now she lived alone without my father, have one of them grab her and hold down her feet and legs while another strangled her to death. Then they could easily bury her in the family grave since no one would ever think of searching there for her body. They know the watchman. It would be the simplest thing to send him off on some errand for an hour or two. Opening up the tomb and dumping her corpse into some old coffin—a grandfather's or some other relative's—would be simple, too. It has been done before. But I will not go into those details, even if I am right in the middle of this dangerous and forbidden revelation, and even if it is only to myself, and even if I am going through some of the most dreadful moments of my life right now.

If this supposition had any basis in fact, if my mother was the one who murdered my father, then they might kill me, too. I am her son, after all. No one has any doubt about that. She carried me, openly, for nine whole months, and didn't try to hide her swollen belly. (Would she have hidden it if she could have? And there were witnesses present at my birth: my grandmother—my father's mother—and the midwife, and other female relatives and neighbors.)

Could my mother have completely changed her mind and decided to no longer accept what accepting the status quo more than forty years ago had produced? And am I, too, one of those rejected products of the status quo? Is that why she didn't tell me about my father's murder? My father is dead now and the page of our past has been turned for good, just like that?

Oh God!

It's a good thing Salwa didn't come over or call. Many a bad thing can turn out to be good. How could I have told her all this? How could I reveal all these horrible thoughts that come into my mind, and all these memories. Wouldn't I have turned instantly into some kind of a freak in her eyes? A monster? How could I ever tell her that my uncle killed his son's young new bride not long after his own young newlywed son was killed. (He became quickly suspicious of her behavior and was worried she would "fall apart." Or maybe he was worried about himself?) He buried her at night, secretly, in the family grave. He opened the old decaying coffin of one of our great grandmothers and shoved her inside, crammed her in, and then locked up the tomb and went back home. Or rather, *they* went back home. They—his brothers, that is—were against him, but they would not abandon their brother, despite their protests against his actions, or rather their complete inability to accept what he had done, but by the time they found out, it was already too late. There was nothing in the world that could keep them apart, and nothing that could make any one of them abandon any of the others. Whenever "the topic" comes up, if it does at all, which is a very rare event indeed and practically non-existent, it comes in the form of symbols and gestures, in such a way that if anyone else were to listen, he or she would not understand a word. An obscure system of extremely common symbols designed not to draw attention or raise anyone's curiosity.

As for the popular version of the story about her, about my cousin's wife, the story goes that she disappeared after her husband was killed. She took off with some man who used to pass through the neighborhood occasionally. The deep sorrow she felt had made a heavy impact on her mind. She had really loved her husband. She was madly in love with him, and he loved her and treated her better than any man has ever treated a wife. She disappeared without a trace. She had no children except for the one already in her womb.

How could I tell all this to Salwa, especially when even without knowing all these things, and after reading no more than the newspaper report, she had decided not to call me. (Did she really make such a decision?) Imagine what her position would be after I told her these stories. Her eyes would probably spin around in their sockets, and she would lose her mind. Then she would leave, slamming the door on her way out to stop me from following her and grabbing her and burying her just like (we) buried my cousin's wife. She'd slam the door on me and my stories and my entire history.

It would not be fair to exchange this history, my history, for hers, even if the purpose was to strengthen our relationship. It would be doubly unfair first because mine is so much weightier than hers, which boils down to a few romances and broken hearts, and her divorce, which is just like every other divorce, no matter how painful. And second, because she wouldn't stay with me for one second after hearing about my history!

Oh God!

Things have a way of changing so suddenly, turning upside down. How did I ever think during times now past, that I was in charge of our relationship, taking or leaving her as I pleased, according to my whims? If I wanted, I could sway things toward marriage, and if I wanted, I could break it off. Or I could keep things just the way they were—regular meetings for rest and relaxation once or twice a week. When Salma discovered I responded to being massaged, she went to a special school and took a three-month course on the art of massage; she bought books and magazines. She still does. She tamed me with her massages. She succeeded in transforming me into "an object" (to my satisfaction) while she massaged me. And while giving me those massages, she would tell me whatever she wanted, knowing I was listening. She knew how to maintain the line that kept me connected to her, and how to strengthen it. So is it the case that once I was a king who ruled on people's needs and requests according to my moods, but now everything has changed, just like in the song by Abd al-Halim Hafez, "The world cast me out, the young prince of princes." (I don't like tears. I don't like anything about humankind except the human brain. The spinal cord. The ability to think. My motto has always been, "I think, therefore I do not cry.")

How would I tell Salwa that my mother, while busy killing my father, never imagined for a moment that news of his murder would only reach me by chance. That my uncles wouldn't tell me, because they think I'm not my father's son, that my father is not my father! And none of my friends over there would want to interfere in a very strange situation they had never heard of before and could hardly comprehend and therefore chose to stay out of it completely and keep quiet, their way of taking cover and hunkering down through the violent assault.

And Salwa would say, "Is that possible?" meaning there was no way my uncles could think that. No way they could think my father was not my father! So how would I tell her they have every reason to think so. Or at least they have their reasons, and their reasons are sound and have a solid basis.

Oh God! Has this subject come up again to destroy my peace of mind, now after forgetting about it for so many years? Ten years. Twenty years. (I had forgotten it!) I never thought it would come back and thrust itself upon me in such a way, with such force, once again! I thought I had been cured of it for good, but here it is, back to burn my insides again and poison my nights and my days. Poison my whole life that I love, that I built, brick by brick, and still continue to build. I have managed to become a part of this milieu where I have been able to find a place for myself. I have become a part of this environment where I can always find my balance, and where I can reach my potential in every aspect and every dimension. So why am I here now, satisfied with my life, and yet still plagued by another place and time?

Did the possibility of such a thing ever cross my mind? That this nightmare would reenter my life with such devastating force?

As for right now, now that the matter has gone this far, and everything that had been suppressed and stifled has exploded, there is no choice but to acknowledge that *a la rigueur je m'enfous*. I really don't give a damn if I am not my father's son! That is the last thing that concerns me now—whether or not I am my father's biological son. I must acknowledge that; it is a matter that no longer concerns me. That's right. I don't care anymore.

All that matters now is that I am "here." I eat and drink and work and love and feel happy and enjoy myself and feel tired and rest and feel sadness and feel joy. I made it through the war in one piece, physically and emotionally. I didn't fall victim to gambling or get addicted to alcohol or drugs. I wasn't wounded or kidnapped. My house was not occupied by militants, nor was I forced to vacate it. And when it was hit by a missile once, I wasn't at home. In fact, I never even got stuck in an elevator even once during twenty years of war and constant sudden interruptions in electricity. I really, really love that so much. It's indescribable. To me it is a clear sign sent from some divine force somewhere in this beautiful and terrible universe telling me that my days are still coming, no doubt about it.

Sometimes I would open the door to the elevator, step inside, and the electricity would go out before the door closed shut. God, that used to give me such faith in the future, and bring such joy to my heart. Other times the lights would suddenly go out and the elevator would stop while I was inside and didn't know what floor we were on, or how far between floors, and when I'd push on the door, it would open and out I would walk onto the very floor I was heading to. I love these sorts of signs that provide exactly what I need. They happened during the war. Like when my house was hit by a missile, as I mentioned earlier, and I had been out only a matter of a few hours. I returned and saw all the damage and imagined what might have happened to me had I been at home. And the time there was a car bomb that exploded right in front of the building where I live. I had just passed by the spot. Only a few minutes later the car exploded. It was loaded with very high explosives. (As it was reported later in the internal security report published in the media in all its forms—written, spoken, and radio broadcast.) The bomb targeted a certain important individual, and it succeeded in hitting him, but it also killed twelve innocent people along with him. People passing by, like me, in that place and at that deadly time. That was a huge and jolting incident, but I was spared. I considered that another one of those signs telling me I would not die during that war. I would be spared, no doubt about it. And I would see many more days to come, beautiful days. Throughout the war, I was absolutely sure, deep down inside, that I would be saved, and that some sort of happiness was waiting for me.

And that's exactly how things turned out. Today I am a satisfied man, happy with everything and about everything in my life. So what is this power that now wants to set me back? That wants to drown me in these matters, in this dirty mess? It is not fair that I should taste the bitterness of the sour grapes my parents ate. No matter how many sour grapes they eat, it is not fair that I should taste the bitterness. I wish I could dye my hair! I wish I could change the color of the hair that I inherited. I wish I could change everything inside me. Everything about me.

I wish I had been born to some other man and woman, in some other religion, with some other accent, from some other place. Why do people thank God for their origins when they have no power to change them? I wish I were a clone like Dolly the Sheep.

I wish that every one of my kinsmen would forget the path that leads to me! But…

But what has been written has been written. No matter how genuinely and how deeply I feel I don't belong to that world, over there, and no matter how much I don't care whether or not I am my father's real son, the validity of this truth cannot be erased or nullified. That matter does not just concern me (I wish that were the case!). It concerns other people, too. Especially other people. For me to say, "What have I got to do with other people?" doesn't mean the problem is solved. They would still be capable (just as they are still) of not calling me to tell me my father is dead, or at least the man I consider to be my father. The man who raised me at least. So why are they— my uncles, I mean—so sure of what they believe? Could they be right to such an extent? Could my mother have possibly hidden such a truth from me? Could my uncles have been so completely sure and yet keep it secret? The reason must be of huge proportion for my mother not to have told me and my uncles not to have told me that my father was killed. They all agreed on it. They all agreed to this evil. That's it. That's exactly it!

I never doubted for a single day that my father was my father, that I was his flesh and blood. Even if the matter did trouble me a lot. So what was it that suddenly came out of me and signaled to my friend at the café to ask me the question that hit me in my most tender spot?

"Are you sure he is your father?"

What he meant was that maybe there was someone else besides my dad—my father I mean—with the same name. But there is no one else in all of Zgharta—in the whole universe in fact—with that name, except my dad and father. I mean except my dad, who is my father.

What exactly was it about me that tipped him off and made him ask that question and make that accusation?

No—I never doubted I was my father's real son, but I used to worry a lot about the idea of a child not being his father's real son. My fear did not extend to the case of adoption. That is totally different. All I mean is this: for a child not to be his father's real son. And it seems to me that is a well-known notion, if not widespread.

These worries spoiled my childhood for me and hurt me. They haunted me for a long time before I got in tune with them and made myself forget them. But they stayed as a burning ember beneath the ashes. What's interesting, curiously enough, is that as kids we were constantly talking about it, from the time we were very small, talking about children who were not their parents' real children. They were very few, but we thought there was at least one or two among us.

That was quite a sensitive subject for me; it would shake up the very foundation of my being whenever anyone would mention it. I never shared in those conversations. Rather, I would withdraw into myself until my friends finished talking about it.

Two of the guys in our group got into an argument once when we were in our early youth. One of them got angry and blurted out, "You're not your father's son!" The other guy just kept on arguing as if he hadn't heard him. Or as if what he heard was just part of their bickering and didn't really carry any weight. As for me, those words fell upon my ears with great impact. To me such words were unbearable, especially since there had been whispers here and there among us to the effect that this particular buddy was not his father's son. I watched with exaggerated concern every move that boy made. I watched him while simultaneously going through the same things with the group as he went through. He was so full of himself. He refused to sit anywhere in a car—this was during the stage of our first experiences with cars—except the front seat, the seat we considered the most prestigious. He worried a lot about his looks and especially his clothes. He was one of the first to smoke in public and one of the first to get married (at age twenty). A few months after him, two other friends followed suit. There was nothing about him that made him special or differentiated him from us. On the contrary, he was very polite and proper. He never bad-mouthed anyone or hurt anyone, and he ingratiated himself to people much more than the rest of us thought was necessary. That really bothered me about him. Sometimes I would attribute it to his deep desire, possibly, for people to like him so much that they would forget his problem. And I was really surprised by how much he looked just like us. Then my surprise would turn into fear sometimes, when it would occur to me that things of this sort—children not being their fathers' sons—happened very easily. *Just like that.* And I would worry about myself, though I never had a single doubt about whether I was my father's son. It was just a general feeling of concern.

I'm not sure if any of my childhood friends ever attributed this possibility to me—that I was not my father's son—but I remember something about my cousin saying it to me one time in a fleeting moment that never repeated itself again afterward.

"And neither are you!"

I think he just said it quickly, if he even said it at all, like saying he was not really saying it. He fell silent the moment it spilled out, trying to hide it. I didn't say a word. I understood his discomfort and guilty feeling to mean not that he had spoken the truth, but that he had just meant to hurt me or insult me. I understood what he said as a swear, like saying, "You bastard!" or something like that.

I read a book once written by a secret service agent whose job it was to censor correspondences of dubious individuals. Sometimes this agent would discover surprising things in those letters. More than once he read letters in which a woman told her lover that she was pregnant and the child was his, not her husband's. He went on to explain how one of these women assured her lover that he was in fact the father of the newly conceived baby because she hadn't slept with her husband in over a month, and the last time she had slept with him (with her husband that is) she was not fertile. Her period had just ended. She remembered that very clearly because she had tried to dissuade him by telling him she still had her period, but he insisted. "That's okay," he said, and then when he discovered during intercourse that her period had actually ended, he asked her why she lied. So she answered that it (her period) had just barely ended, which was true, but he didn't believe her. Then in another letter she told her lover that she had made a final decision not to abort the baby, and not to tell her husband the truth, because he did not suspect anything and in spite of everything she wanted to keep her family together. She also said her husband was a good man with many good qualities, even though their sex life was awful (even disgusting sometimes), for he did not excite her, and she did not experience the least bit of pleasure with him.

I was a young boy when I came across that book and read it. How did I happen to come upon it? Indeed, how did it find its way to me? I don't know! It is one of those childhood books I still keep on my bookshelf to this day. Why haven't I thrown it away the way I have thrown away so many other books I used to keep by reason of *fetichisme*.

Well, anyway. That is a subject I decided to forget about a long time ago. I am finished with it. It is no longer a recurring nightmare that comes back every time I think of it. That's it! I'm here now, in Beirut, and I want to live my life as it should be. And really, everything has helped me to forget—everything I see and hear and touch. Really. Everything. I will never forget, for example, something my mother said once that impressed me. One time when I was misbehaving and really giving her trouble all day long, she said: "You really are your father's son, aren't you? Otherwise you would not give me so much trouble all the time. And I wouldn't have" (here's the clincher!) "agonized so much on the day of your birth." Salma told me, when she told me about her previous desire to get pregnant from the man she fell in love with before divorcing her husband, that it was the most splendid joy for a woman to become pregnant by a man she loved, and the child, no matter what happened later, would always be the child of that joy. In other words, in such a case a woman would be able to bear all the pains of childbirth with complete acceptance and in the best emotional spirit and attitude.

Hearing that really helped me to forget. Hearing my mother say that reassured me. The important thing is that I forgot, and for all practical purposes these things did not bother me for a very long time. If they did come up, they left as quickly as they came and without leaving a trace. There was no alternative but for me to forget, because it is not easy at all to live with such a nightmare. And it truly was a nightmare that I lived with night and day sometimes. At night I would recall what had happened during the day, and anything that had something to do with that subject, trying to reconstruct my parents' lives, one piece at a time. I used to imagine myself in their place, and consider in detail what I would have done if it were me. I would imagine new things as my awareness increased. And at every stage of my growing awareness I would recompose my parents' lives, incorporating the new bits of information I had obtained.

From as far back as I can remember, I listened for any bit of information on the subject, and I recorded each item in my memory, keeping them at the forefront of my thoughts, just behind my eyes, so I would not forget them for a second. I did this day and night, and they even entered into my dreams, too. And unfortunately for me there were lots of these bits of information, indeed more than a person can bear, starting from the beginning, the very beginning, with the way my parents got married. Actually, even before that, starting with the note someone tossed to my mother when she was just a young girl of fifteen. I used to listen so carefully, paying close attention to every single detail and comment, picking up bits and pieces here and there. Some story my grandmother told, a comment by my father, a gesture from my uncle or a relative or a friend, and Maryam. Most of all Maryam. I would fill in the holes and missing pieces with other information I had managed to obtain or had figured out so the story would be complete and not full of blanks. Each year as I grew older I would recreate the events from the beginning, adding in whatever new pieces I had gleaned through new information and experience. It became a kind of obsession or addiction that I couldn't get control of until I went off to college, settled in Beirut, and my visits and connections to the village started to decrease. In this respect the war, which lasted a long time and made it unsafe to travel and nearly impossible to make phone calls, was helpful to me.

But I always thought, especially when I was young, that these were my own problems and these suspicions mine alone. And I also thought that they were problems based on facts and scenes that no one else noticed, or at least that no one remembered, no one who had been a part of it all, or had some interest in it, in particular that note that "someone" tossed to my mother while she bathed, and what was written on it, and then the way my mother later married my father, and the way I was born, and the way they neglected to choose a name for me. I honestly believed that such matters were long forgotten (or at least I hoped so). And I also thought that what went on between my parents before they got married and afterward went unnoticed by anyone. I thought I was the only one who kept track of those matters, the only one who dredged them up, the only one who suffered from them. Everyone else was ignorant of them or had forgotten them, most of all my uncles. Of course I said to myself from time to time that my uncles must have some idea, or maybe more than that, about everything, but they kept quiet about it. Indeed they forgot about it so no one would take note and cause things to take on more importance than they deserved. But now my suspicions aren't suspicions anymore. Now I am certain. They are completely aware of what was and what came to be. They know every detail, including the ones I don't know myself. And that's why they are treating me like someone who has nothing to do with the fact of my father's murder.

It is entirely unreasonable that they would have only "some idea," as I used to think. That's completely illogical. They must know every detail. In fact, they must have lived the entire story from beginning to end, and were part of it, helped create it. Could they possibly not have known that when I was born, my grandmother—their mother and my father's mother—was the one who named me that name—Rashid—a whole week after my birth?

It is totally unreasonable to think they did not know that. But I always believed they wanted to forget it, and that their will to forget was very strong, judging by the way they behaved as if it never existed, it never happened. I was convinced that I was the only one who lived that nightmare. And it was also my belief that whereas they avoided the situation, I dredged it up and let it feed my anxiety and give birth to burning questions. But things did not work out the way I imagined, or at least not the way I hoped.

What had been my uncles' position when I went a whole week without a name? What did they say to my father, and what did he say to them?

Why did I spend a whole week without a name? Why didn't my mother worry about a name for me? And my father, didn't he want to give me a name? I suppose I was not their pride and joy, then, nor did I bring happiness into their hearts. Not into either of their hearts! Why? Was I some mistake whose consequences they didn't want to have to bear?

But it was my grandmother herself who proudly tells the story of how my father came in one week after my birth (one week!) and examined me closely, then declared that I was his son. His flesh and blood!

And so my mother was stuck, like a "stick in the mud." I was her flesh and blood and she could not deny that. After all, she carried me in her womb openly, so all the world could see, for nine long months. She gave birth to me at home, not in the hospital (where I might have been switched), in the presence of the midwife and her mother and my father's mother and others. And still others were waiting outside.

My father left the task of naming me to whomever wanted it. And my mother never even considered the matter herself, not before and not after. Besides, after I was born, she wasn't in any condition to think about choosing a name, because she was in a very bad state. She had severe hemorrhaging during delivery, which was not a surprise to her—she expected exactly that. She did not hesitate to mention it, with shocking openness, whenever she talked about the birth. That made me want to curl up inside myself and hide I don't know where. Sometimes Maryam would call to me, when her conversations with my mother reached these sensitive topics, and wrap her arms around me and kiss me.

I didn't know if I liked Maryam or not, but I felt she was a part of me. As if she had had something to do with my making, from the beginning, for better or for worse. I enjoyed her presence, even if it did entail the daunting amount of information that my mother poured into her possession. Later, when I grew older and became a young man, I began to wonder if she would keep all that information to herself, after she got married. And with much worry I would wonder if she really was capable of keeping such things from her husband, or even wanted to. I was very concerned about who it would be who would marry her. I never ever thought it would be my youngest uncle. When I found out about her marriage, to my youngest uncle in particular, I was stunned. I ran home to tell my mother and say to her in an uproar barely able to catch my breath, "Mom! Maryam is going to marry my uncle!" All my mother said, with complete calm, was, "I wish her all the best."

This answer really shocked me, because I thought I was revealing to her my biggest secret, and was revealing to her that now I, too, shared the same trench and we should face the future as a team. I believed our best interests had become one and the same, and we could put our heads together.

I was very worried, because the depth of the friendship between Maryam and my mother provided some comfort, but only to a point.

I don't know what Maryam's feelings toward me were, whether she liked me or not, or whether she felt sorry for me or full of disdain. It was really important to me to know what I was to her. Sometimes I imagined how she might tell someone my story, especially her husband to be. I would try to guess what she might say, and wondered about it.

Now, at my current age, if I could chance to meet up with her while she was still at that age, I am certain that I would grab her and hold her tight. In my mind and in my subconscious she is the woman I desire. I want her. The first time I ever masturbated and made myself ejaculate was over her. What happened was, she was at our house, and I was just reaching puberty. She was in the living room, stretched out on the sofa and waiting for my mother to return from some errand, I don't remember exactly what anymore. It was summer time. Some time in the afternoon, and I was in my bedroom, the place I went to sleep and be alone with my personal things. I knew she was there, but I wasn't sure if she was aware of my presence in my room. At one point I looked through the keyhole of my door to see why it was so quiet inside the house, and I saw her there sprawled out on the couch, her head propped up on the armrest and her bottom resting on the edge of the seat.

Her hand was between her thighs right where they are joined. Her dress was raised up to her thighs allowing her panties to show somewhat clearly, but her hand was scratching at the lower part of her belly over her dress in a very calm and slow manner. She opened her eyes from time to time, as if reluctantly, in order to avoid being surprised by someone walking in on her in that position. I was aroused by what I saw, and during that period of time I had just begun my first experiences with touching my body. Out of the blue I opened the door quietly. Surely she saw me open the door, or sensed it, or realized it on some level, but she didn't stop or change what she was doing one bit, not the way she reluctantly opened her eyes from time to time, as if to watch for my mother's sudden return or my father's or anyone else's, nor in the way she lay on the couch with total abandon, nor in the way she moved her hand. And so I was amazed, which aroused me even more. I remained standing there at the door, not advancing or retreating. I stood there watching her without fear or shame. Then I don't know where I got the boldness or how—indeed I don't know if you can call it boldness—but I stood at the door facing inside my room which was dimmer than the living room, and I brought out that thing whose significance I had only recently begun to discover, and started stroking it with my hand, up and down, according to my desire and delight, until I ejaculated a clear liquid that was white and sticky.

That was the first time I ever came in such a direct, complete, and consummate way. After I came and got a good look, I noticed her eyes were still shut. She wasn't opening them anymore, and it seemed to me that her eyelids at that time were very heavy. Much heavier than before. I withdrew into my room without a word or a gesture or anything else. I shut the door behind me very quietly and lay on my bed. I felt victorious. That was the first emotion that came to mind as I lay there resting and thinking deeply and clearly. And I felt I was a lucky person.

I had triumphed over my fears concerning her marriage to my uncle. (What happened between us took place during the period of "negotiations" that after a few months led up to her marrying him.) I had triumphed over my fear because what happened between us was sex;

it was intercourse. I had sex with her. No, more than that, for she was obligated to look after me. She was obligated to curb the desire, if she had it, to divulge secrets that could be harmful to me. And furthermore, her having accepted what happened, her having brought it on in fact, meant that she accepted me to a certain extent as her master. I mean she accepted my dominance. Yes! My dominance. What I had on her was akin to what a master has over his slave. And since she accepted my dominance in the absence of marriage or anything similar to marriage, then that meant her estimation of me was extremely high.

So I am my father's son.

And, to put it bluntly, if she dared tell anyone her secrets, I would not hesitate one second to tell mine. I wouldn't be shy about it in the least. I'd go directly to my uncle and tell him, "You'd better be careful, Uncle. Don't marry this woman. She is not honorable! Listen to what happened between her and me…" and I'd be sure to mention a certain mark on her body, in a place no one sees unless she herself shows him. But I remembered that I didn't see anything special on the parts of her body I had seen, like a mole or a burn scar or any kind of scar or vaccination, or anything of the sort, and so I wouldn't be able to support my claim with irrefutable evidence, because I didn't see anything but the color of her underpants and the section of her bared thighs. That is not something that points clearly to some special, personal characteristic of a particular woman. Every woman has underpants and every woman has bare thighs. So I decided I should get closer next time, get closer to her and touch her and squeeze her. Even more than that, like a man and a woman like my buddies tell me, and if possible I should make her reciprocate. That way she couldn't just say whatever suited her and I would no longer be threatened by her ability to tell, along with whatever extra secrets she wanted to throw in about me that my mother had told her.

And so I set about planning and watching for the right opportunity, but the opportunities wouldn't present themselves. In fact, it was a long time after that before she came back to visit us. Every day that passed made it all the harder to wait. At last I asked my mother why Maryam hadn't visited in such a long time, which surprised my mother. She said that Maryam was busy getting ready for the wedding. Actually, she said only that she was busy.

Maryam's marriage bothered my mother without a doubt, but she didn't have any excuse or strategy for preventing it or standing in its way. As for my explanation for Maryam's absence, it was very different from my mother's. Maryam hadn't visited because she was embarrassed by me. It was too hard for her to see me after what had happened between her and me. Eventually her visits resumed and became regular, although there were longer gaps between them because of her involvement in wedding plans. And with her return came my renewed sense of hope. I started inventing ways to allow our bodies to touch or rub up against each other. I would stand in the doorway, for example, as she passed through it so she would touch me and her body would encompass me. Or I would stand behind her to reach something high up in front of her and that kind of thing. She would turn bright red and I would worry my mother would see me. She was the first woman I fantasized about, and my fantasies of her accompanied me whenever I was by myself. Once I saw her through the keyhole of my bedroom door all alone in the living room, so I opened the door and stood in the doorway, just as I had the last time. She got up immediately and caught up with my mother who was making coffee in the kitchen. As for my last attempt, it was much worse than that one: she was crouched down looking for one of my mother's slippers under the bed. I approached under the pretense of helping her and leaned down very low to see under the bed, but I turned my head toward her. I was in a position to see everything and see everything I did. And I reached out with my hand to touch her in all those places, but she flinched as if scorched by a flame and ran off after slapping me and cursing me. She said, "You pig!" To me that was unbearable. I was extremely discouraged. I couldn't get over it for many days and regretted what I had done more than words can say. It wasn't just a feeling of guilt, but a feeling that I had plundered what had taken me weeks to win. And that's what mattered most, for now there was no longer anything to prevent her from spilling anything she wanted, whenever she wanted.

She made a point to make that clear to me. What happened that day never happened at all in her eyes. She never saw me take out my "thing," and as for what she was doing, it was nothing more than scratching an itch, something she had every right to do when she was all alone. And besides, she couldn't even remember for sure if she had scratched anything because she was asleep. She was sleeping. I intruded. It was in my best interest to keep quiet. How stupid I was! How could I have relinquished my victory to her, the victory I never dreamed of winning. Why didn't I think it over? Why didn't I figure in the possibility that she might refuse? I should have taken it slower. I should have been satisfied with doing things like standing in the doorway and forcing her to rub her body up against me, or like standing behind her to reach for something up high in front of her, or other things like that. But I lost the whole war, not just a battle, so now I had to forget that phase entirely and move on to something else, whatever that was. One thing was sure, that trump card I once held in my hand was gone forever. Never again could I dream of getting it back.

Soon she would be my youngest uncle's wife, the uncle my father loved most of all. I wasn't worried that she would tell my uncle about anything I had done, because she was very sharp, not the type to make blunders. And after all, she knew that if she ever plunged into a battle with me she wouldn't win. She stood to get very hurt, no matter how much I lost. (Oh God! My uncles would say, "If he were one of us, of our flesh and blood, he wouldn't have done such a thing!") However, I did worry she would tell my mother. Who knew how it might unfold, especially in the absence of anything to prevent it? Nothing would prevent Maryam from dispensing, if she felt like it, that huge and momentous store of information my mother had provided her with (with me listening). My mother emptied out to her everything that was in her soul and in her heart and everything related. She emptied out to her what should have been left untold. It is not wise to reveal everything, nor is it wise to be off one's guard and end up handing over one's soul like that. Nor is it wise to forget one's shame to such an extent.

My mother told her that it had been no surprise to her whatsoever that she nearly died giving birth to me. (My mother claims that she almost died, but my grandmother— her mother—and my other grandmother—my father's mother—said the delivery was difficult because it was her first.) Nor was my mother surprised that she suffered a lot of hemorrhaging, because throughout her pregnancy she felt as though a huge rock were growing inside her and that the rock would tear her apart on its way out. For her the biggest shock the day of my birth was that she lived through it and didn't die.

On her wedding night, after my father poured out his anger onto her, my mother dreamed she was in the desert and it was long ago, in the pre-Islamic times when tribes attacked each other. One tribe attacked the tribe she belonged to and captured her. The horseman she ended up with raped her early in the evening after forcing her to lie down on the hot sand and pebbles. She wished she could die or take revenge on him somehow, but she was a powerless captive who could do nothing but mull over her anger. When he got up off her she stood and went to a pile of rocks that were hot from the long day under the sun. She slipped her bare feet into the pile, hoping there might be a scorpion that would bite her, or a poisonous snake. In the dream my mother was in love with her cousin, as young Arab girls were in those days, and she would have married him in a few days had she not ended up with that strange wild animal. She started dreaming that whenever her captors were away she would meet her cousin, and she wished she would never wake up from this dream.

My mother bled so much while trying to deliver me that a doctor was sought who recommended rushing her to the hospital. She went and I was left at home and was not taken outside at all. A few days after I was born, while my mother was still in the hospital, and my father had not yet seen me, my grandmother on my father's side named me. Rashid. I don't know why that name. No one in the family ever had that name. She was quite taken with the famous Abassid Caliph Harun al-Rashid and was always telling us his stories, which she also loved.

My father did not see me until a whole week after my birth, and no one found that to be surprising, especially not my grandmother, who was famous for knowing more about men than men knew about themselves. To the point that women sometimes asked her if she weren't actually a man herself at one time. And my mother, of course, was not at all surprised either, for reasons that were at the very heart of the problem.

When he came to see me for the first time, my father examined me closely and for a long time. A very long time. I was a very beautiful baby, unusually beautiful. So beautiful a father could not help but be proud to have me as a son. My mother left the room before my father came to see me; my grandmother on my father's side, however, stayed in the room after backing up to the doorway to inspect her son, my father.

My father pulled up a chair and sat down to inspect me and observe me. After a while his friends came looking for him (my father was always accompanied by friends). They were surprised to see him sitting like that, unlike himself, and so they asked him if there was something wrong. "I'm memorizing every bit of him," he answered, standing up. "He is indeed my son!"

What was my father thinking when he said that? What was going through his mind? Was he just stating the obvious, so my grandmother would hear and rejoice the way people rejoice when they hear the self-evident spoken? Or did he know that his mother held some doubts and he wanted to give her peace of mind and give her the green light to go ahead and care for me as she should. I mean, as she should care for his legitimate son.

(Would my father have had DNA testing done the way they do today, to determine if he was truly my biological father? I could ask myself the same question. Shall I have DNA testing done to determine if I am his son? And what difference would the results of such a test make?)

He asked her where she got that name, and she said, "Don't you like it?" and he was silent.

Did his friends know the details of his relationship with my mother and therefore understand the underlying meaning of what he had said, or did they merely understand the superficial meaning, which was that he was inspecting his firstborn son who would carry his name, his newborn son who amazed him and filled his heart with pride and joy.

What did my father see in me that resembled him and reassured him so completely that he decided my mother should stay in his home and take care of me? I am sure that his reassurance after seeing me was the decisive factor in his decision not to hurt her. (I am talking about hurting her in a huge way, as in killing her and hiding her body somewhere.) It was also a factor in his decision to keep her in his house, which is why, I suppose, my mother sees me as the cause of her misery. If not for me things might have gone differently and led eventually to her rescue. Who knows? Anyway, what could be worse than the kind of life she ended up with?

It seems my father could not help himself at some point, while he was bent over me and taking a careful look, from opening up my diaper and making a close inspection of what had been hidden under it. He took a big sigh of relief when he caught sight of something (a birthmark?) on a particular spot on my body that was exactly like something on a particular spot of his body. My mother was surprised when she returned and saw that my diaper was still unfastened. She screamed without thinking, loud enough for my father to hear, and so he came back and said, "Leave him alone!"

My mother glanced back at him, merely responding to the direction from which the voice came, nothing more, and continued in my direction.

"I told you to leave him alone!" my father shouted.

She looked at him again, confused and trying to understand, and then he slapped her. Then he picked her up with his strong hands and pushed her out the door. At that moment I began to cry, most likely from having been hit myself by some of that violence, because my mother was holding me and trying to put my clothes back on. Undoubtedly, she was forced to let me fall from her hands quickly, and so I fell onto the edge of the bed and started to scream. My mother does not scream. She didn't scream at all when my father slapped her and shoved her out of the room though she tried to stop him. Had it not been for the sound my father made when he ordered her to leave me alone, and had it not been for the sound of his hand hitting her face, the whole scene might have been like a silent movie. And just as she didn't scream, neither did she cry. Crying was something she simply would not let happen, no matter what. "Hamad D. will never make me cry!" Sure he had destroyed her life, but he would never have the satisfaction of seeing a single tear fall from her eyes.

My sudden scream brought my grandmother into the room, and there she saw her son pushing my mother so harshly. My mother was still healing from her wounds, which really called for staying longer in the hospital, but for some reason—concern for me, no doubt—she had checked out and assured the doctor she had people at home who would take care of her.

My grandmother saw her son throw my mother to the ground, and she saw my mother head toward the sofa to throw herself onto it, and my grandmother also saw my father's buddies standing there silently, waiting quietly and casually for my father to finish what he was doing so they could all leave together, as if my father had asked them to wait a minute while he went to get his keys or something.

Right up until her death, my grandmother insisted that women are evil inside and out, but she also always added that men are more evil than women. "Men are mules," she used to say. A mule in this context stands for hardness and boorishness and selfishness and lack of gratitude. The epitome of ingratitude, as if the concept of gratitude were non-existent. The one flaw my grandmother found in my mother was her fickleness the few days before their marriage. My father's shock the morning after their wedding did not go unnoticed by my grandmother. She guessed right away what the reason was, just as she realized that night had been the entrance of both of them into hell.

If it were not our custom to check for the spot of blood on the bridal couple's bedsheet the morning after their first night together, then recklessness on the part of the bride could lead to worse things. My grandmother is firm on that matter.

My grandmother loved me the way grandmothers love their grandchildren and then some. Whenever she saw me, she usually said, "You're the spitting image of your father. You look so much like him. Thank God!"

And she also saw a strong resemblance between my gestures and actions and my father's, which also made her very happy. "The exact same gestures!" she used to say.

When he hit her that time, my grandmother said to my mother, "Listen. Hamad is my son, and there is no one in this world I love more than him, but I'm warning you from this day forward, watch out! Surely he thinks you have sullied his son. You have stained his son's entrance into the world. Lots of men think that, all over the world. It is up to you to do something to curb his anger—but I don't know what."

My mother did not say anything in response to what my grandmother said, and my grandmother did not bring up the subject again at all, openly or otherwise. They shared a sort of friendship based on one another's mutual adherence to boundaries. I am certain that my grandmother knew about everything, without anyone having told her. She was extremely intelligent and had a keen intuition that penetrated right to the heart of things. Once, when I brought up the matter of my being an only child, she said to me, swearing upon all my relatives and friends, "And that is how you will remain! That is your fate!" Then she came closer to me, hugging me tight, and said, "Come to my heart, little boy who is just like his father."

After I was born, my mother started having dreams about me. I became an obstacle between her and her cousin, the one she dreamed of meeting in a tent outside the village of the one who had taken her captive. She also dreamed once that I had become a thirteen-year-old young man and had become suspicious of that other man, and so I asked her who he was and why he had come. My questions frightened her. She saw it as a bad omen. She told her cousin about her fears and told him they must find a way to deal with this youngster, otherwise he would prevent them from meeting with each other, which was something she could not bear. Her cousin told her he could not bear that either. "I would rather suffer death than be forbidden from seeing you. I am prepared to do anything to protect our relationship." Then they discussed the matter at great length but could not find a solution. Then one day, as worry nearly got the better of them, he said to her, "Leave it to me. I will find the right solution." And so it was. Her cousin slyly got acquainted with the boy (me, that is), talked to him and gained his trust. Then one day he coaxed the boy into accompanying him on a hunting trip to the furthest and highest regions of the desert. At night they slept in the same tent. The man sat up to see if the boy was sleeping, and the boy woke up immediately and asked the man, "Why did you sit up?"

"I heard a noise outside," he answered.

"Go back to sleep," the boy said. "There's nothing outside."

So the man lay back down again and pretended to fall asleep in order to put the boy at ease so he would fall asleep. After a while, the man very delicately and quietly picked up some dirt and threw it into the distance in order to make sure the boy was asleep. And with that the boy woke up in alarm, as if he had heard an explosion. He grabbed the man by the neck and said, "Go back to sleep or I'll kill you!" And so the man gave up his plans for the time being and they continued their excursion together, until they caught sight of a huge fire off in the distance. They went closer until they could make out two animals the man recognized, for he knew their owners. Previously he had met up with them on his trips into the desert and had seen them up close. He saw the way they pursued their prey, be it animal or man, for they were more like ferocious wolves than human beings. "Perfect," he said to himself. "I will never get a better opportunity than this." So he said to the boy, "Go and get those two donkeys. I'll stay behind and make sure no one surprises you." And off the boy went to carry out the man's request. He went directly to the two donkeys, guided by the light of the fire near them, and when he got to his destination, two big scary men pounced on him. But before they could grab him, he took hold of their heads, one head in each hand, and slammed them into each other. They fell to the ground, dead. Then he untied the two donkeys and led them back to where the man was waiting for him. When he arrived he said, "Take the donkeys! You were trying to get me, but you will not get away next time!" The man gave up trying, because any new attempt would certainly lead to his own demise. That boy was not completely human; he was part jinn, too, no doubt. The man decided they would go back, but on the way something unexpected happened. The boy asked if they could stop so he could take care of something—move his bowels, in fact—so the man stopped for him and waited for him in the shade provided by the donkey. But the boy was taking a long time, so the man called to him. The boy didn't answer, so the man got worried the boy might be setting him up. He called to him a second time, but still the boy didn't answer. With extreme caution, the man approached the small sand hill behind which the boy had ducked to relieve himself, and when he was able to see around to the other side of it, there was the boy, lying on the ground, his whole body puffed up and swollen, his hand thrust into a hole up to his shoulder. The man, in shock, came closer to the boy and dragged him out until his hand appeared, still clutching a huge snake which had been strangled to death. The snake had bitten him, but before its poison took effect, the boy had reached into its snake hole, grabbed it by the head and strangled it to death before dying himself.

My mother's dreams were woven like tales out of ancient Arab folklore, and those of pre-Islamic times in particular. Those were the stories she loved most as a young schoolgirl. She read them with an insatiable passion and appetite.

Even though my mother had such dreams, which revealed her desire to be rid of me, she did not actually hate me. They were merely the kind of dreams not worth asking about, dreams that would come whenever the tremendous pressure she was under day and night caused her to doze off. My mother was living a life that was not her own, a life she didn't like. She was living the life of some other woman. "It's as though I am not my own self," she used to say to Maryam. "As though the real me were stowed away in some closet somewhere or placed on some forgotten shelf!" I don't know if Maryam really understood what my mother was saying, or if it was even possible for her to understand the depth of my mother's pain, of her anguish, of her torment. Because my mother, in spite of her love for Maryam, and her total confidence in her, would repeat from time to time, "No one can walk in another person's shoes."

What my mother hated about me was the fact that I was my father's son; she didn't hate me personally. Actually, she loved me. If I were the same person and my father were some other man my mother loved, there would not have been any problem, and she would not have dreamed those harmful dreams. She said to me once, after the murder of a young man in the village saddened her and upset her, "I wish you could stay young forever." That was so I could be safe from the type of killing that grown-ups, not children, were exposed to. She cared for me like the most caring of mothers and more. My clothes were always clean, cleaner than those of all the kids I played with. My friends always envied me for the good lunches I brought to school. Sometimes they would come out and say things like, "Lucky you, you're an only child." And like all mothers, she would tell cute and funny stories about me. She said that once I snuck up behind my father, who was in the bathroom urinating, thrust my hand between his legs, and grabbed the stream of urine as it came down! (My father didn't actually tell my mother about this incident directly. She heard it from him as he was telling it to his mother, my grandmother.)

She used to tell this story and laugh with all her heart. Then she would hold me close to her and hug me to her chest and kiss me hard. And whenever I had a fever, she would not sleep. She would get up every so often to check my forehead with her hand or with her lips when she wasn't sure if her hand was accurate. She would listen to my breathing to see if it was regular, and check my color to see if I was flushed. She was an ideal mother in that respect, and some of the neighbors complimented her for this and pointed out to my father how lucky he was to have her. Thanks to her help, I was sometimes one of the top students in class and always one of the good ones. My mother was especially good at reading and writing, including reading and writing in French. She also knew some English.

She had attended the St. Lazarus Nuns' School. She loved school and was always the first or second in her class. She passed the Certificate exam on the first try and the Brevé exam on the first try, with wonderful grades, when a lot of students failed and had to repeat the school year. She loved the Arabic language a lot, and if it hadn't been for her desire to strengthen her French, she would never have considered reading a book in any other language. She loved stories from ancient Arabic books, especially the ones about generosity, chivalry, loyalty, and most of all, love.

My mother always dreamed of falling in love first and then getting married. "Was that too much to ask, Maryam? Was it? Was I asking for too much?" Maryam would fall silent and roll her eyes before answering, "What girl does not wish for the same thing?"

"Don't ever get married without falling in love." That was my mother's advice to Maryam. (Was my mother worried that Maryam might marry her youngest brother-in-law? No doubt the possibility crossed her mind. With her sharp intelligence, she could see that the two of them shared a small arena, and their getting together was not only possible, but highly probable.) "I'm getting older," Maryam would answer. "And my choices are dwindling. I have to cut down on my demands."

"Mine is a different story," my mother would mumble as though to herself, especially since she got married at an age when she had the full right to be demanding. She was seventeen years old, very smart in school, knew everything there was to know about the cinema—names of movies, actors, and actresses. She used to go to the movies once a week (where she met Anwar secretly for sure). Her parents did not object to her going to the cinema, even though her father was not too keen on the idea. Her mother got excited hearing her daughter rattle off those strange names and tell those strange stories. She would tell her mother the whole story of the film she saw, from beginning to end. And her mother would get so excited that she would allow her to go to the cinema sometimes without even asking for her father's permission. "On condition," her mother would say. "On condition you tell me the whole story without leaving anything out." My mother, however, would gloss over the romantic scenes, summarizing it with a kiss. "And he kissed her," she would say to her mother. "Right in front of you?" my grandmother would ask in amazement, in complete astonishment. "You mean nothing separated them from you?"

My mother used to buy all the movie star magazines, cut out their pictures, and tuck them into all her books and notebooks. My mother was very beautiful, and still is. It seems that the young man, Anwar, the one she fell in love with, was of the same type, at least in terms of his extracurricular interests. He loved cinematography and photography. In fact, he opened a photo shop, where he also sold movie star magazines and pictures of famous actors and actresses. It also seems that my mother at that time was at the peak of being in love with him and crazy about him. There is no doubt that the two pictures that I have in my possession are from that particular period. They were shot in a photography studio without question, which is clear from the backdrop behind my mother, the solid colored carpeting, and the lighting that required special equipment, and most of all my mother's pose, which required a private setting in which the subject could be free to pose in that manner.

These two pictures that I have were not taken in Hollywood or New York or Paris or London or any western capital. They were taken in Zgharta in the early fifties or in the late forties. Yes, when it was considered unusual and unimaginable for girls to swim, and when the women of the village were wrapped in black mourning clothes, due to the many young men who were killed in the blood-revenge disputes that flared up during that period and spilled over even more into the next. Dozens fell victim to those vendetta slayings. That was also the time when a young woman's elopement or marriage against her parents' will led to an all-out war against the young man, causing the village elders and religious leaders to step in to try to resolve matters with whatever solutions they could muster.

My mother appeared in the two pictures half naked!

How could she? Was her friend able to influence her to such an extent? Did she surrender to him so completely and pose half naked for him because he convinced her that he would marry her whenever she said the word? Wasn't she worried that those pictures might fall into some stranger's hand or some relative's? What would have happened if they had fallen into her father's hands, for example, or her mother's? Or the neighbor's? Or the neighborhood children's or her classmates'? Was my mother that careless? Did my father know these pictures existed? My mother brought them with her to his house and hid them there. Didn't my father ever find them by chance while looking for some thing or another? The whole thing is really strange and hard to believe.

Or was it that my mother was suicidal in a sense, unconcerned about what might happen to her, even if it meant her total ruin.

Or maybe she actually had been seeking such ruin from the very beginning, which to her was not ruin at all, but rather a means of escaping from a prison in which she could not bear to be sentenced for life. Otherwise there is no way to explain her leaving those pictures in the house even if well hidden, for she appeared in those pictures half naked! Wearing nothing but a slip. And in one of them, she was standing up, while in the other she was sitting on the floor with her thighs exposed seductively. (And had he taken other pictures that were even more daring? It was clear that my mother was ready for any adventure with him. Had they had some pictures taken together and then torn them up after looking them over first? Or does he still have them somewhere?) My mother was living the madness of her youth.

I could never look at those pictures for very long before I had to look away. There was a force or something that always made me turn away. It was my mother for certain in those pictures, and it was not easy for me, even until very recently, to even contemplate that my mother could also be a woman. And I don't believe it is easy for anyone I know or associate with or anyone I have ever known or ever associated with to consider that his mother could also be a woman. I could never figure out how there could be people who had mothers who worked in less respectable milieus. I wondered a lot about their relationships with their mothers, how they felt about them deep inside, and whether it bothered them, and to what extent.

There was nothing spontaneous in those two pictures except for my mother. I mean that everything in those pictures was carefully planned ahead of time, except for that striking spontaneity that emanated from my mother. In one of the pictures my mother is standing in the center. Her photographer-producer friend taking the picture had been trying to fully capture the Hollywood figure he saw in her. My mother stuck out her chest, displaying its full shape, as far as she could. (By her chest I mean her breasts.) She is standing on one leg with the other leg raised like someone about to take a step. She is looking straight into the camera without any hesitation. She is standing on a rug, not a carpeted floor. In the other picture she is sitting on the very same rug with the same patterns and designs as the first picture. In the picture my mother's face is radiant, beaming with happiness and delight as if paradise were right there behind the door and all she had to do was push it open. She is sitting on the rug posing in a manner the photographer-producer wanted in order to show all the female charms a woman could possibly display in a magazine in those days. My mother appears to yield completely to the photographer's demands without the slightest doubt or concern or resistance or fear. There is only the tiniest look of surprise that can barely be detected, the kind of surprise of someone who innocently does something unexpected. The photographer had peeled her left bra strap down over her shoulder, baring the upper part of her breast and showing clearly the beginning of her cleavage. He had told her to sit with one leg stretched out and the other bent at the knee, and to lift her slip and tuck it between her thighs, which were bare all the way to her hip. Did her friend photograph her in that particular way in order to send the pictures to some movie agency? Did he convince her there was a good chance some producer would be interested and might even offer her a role in Egypt or in America, in Hollywood itself? I bet that was it. Why else would she have that passport that I found among her things, with an Egyptian visa stamped on it? Wasn't that proof? Undeniable proof? So why did my mother get a passport, and why a visa to Egypt? And indeed, the bigger question was, how had she managed to do all that without my father's permission, since under Lebanese law a woman can only obtain a passport with her husband's written consent! How was my mother able to accomplish all that? Who helped her, and why? I know.

I know that she did not reveal it even to her closest friend Maryam! I never heard her say a single word to her about it. The topic never crossed her lips at any time or in any place. But the passport is right here before me with a visa to Egypt stamped right on it. I found it when I was in the attic looking for some things of mine. My mother was at home at the time, but she didn't seem at all concerned about what I might find, or what articles of hers she needed to keep secret. The whole thing was just like her marriage to my father, after her disappointment over her friend Anwar. It was also just like her half-naked pictures that she hid at home, and like the way she did not even try to explain to my father that she had lost her virginity to someone before him, or like the way she tried to cover up for that by going through an operation to restore her hymen to its previous condition, something that was rarely done in our country in those days, but was possible.

I know that my mother's friend Anwar had emigrated to America via Egypt. It seems he wanted to try his luck in the movies, but he did not succeed for some reason. Perhaps it was the whole atmosphere surrounding acting in those days, after the October revolution and the regime of President Gamal Abd al-Nasser. There's no doubt that Anwar left Cairo for the United States, where he is still living and owns a pretty decent store somewhere in New Jersey, where he has relatives. He does not work in the movies in Hollywood, and does not even live in California. It seems he didn't have much luck fulfilling the dreams of his youth and childhood. Was it, I wonder, my mother's beauty that made him plunge into that artistic venture, and then once he had some distance from it, from my mother's beauty that is, the spell was broken and he reverted to pursuing other more mundane and serious matters? Did his relatives sit him down and say, "Listen. People here have to work in order to have a decent life. If all you want to do is stay out until all hours of the night, wake up in the middle of the afternoon, and waste your time reading expensive magazines, then go back to Lebanon! If there's some other work you want, go get it for yourself. But this is all we have to offer you!"

And so it seems, going back to the question of my mother's passport and visa to Egypt, that it was Anwar who did that, by mutual agreement with my mother. The passport photo was from his own studio, no doubt about that, because my mother appears in that picture exactly the same as she did in the two other pictures that I spoke about, with the same haircut, the same number of loose hairs dangling from the rest of the hair that was combed over her forehead. And a slight imperfection in the film that appears in both pictures as a line on her left cheek. And the white necklace she was wearing. And other details that leave no doubt whatsoever that they were in agreement and that he would go ahead of her to work things out. The visa was from the Egyptian embassy in Beirut. He must have gotten her visa when he got his own. He traveled to Egypt during the same period my mother received her visa. This is clear from the dates, and it doesn't take much intelligence or brains to figure that out. Then he must have traveled to Egypt before her, hoping to find a job of course and to find a place for them to stay. There is no doubt that the agreement was that he would signal her to come once he rented an apartment and furnished it adequately. Life in Egypt in those days was not very expensive, and he had enough to stay there for some time without work, especially since he came from a relatively well-to-do family. But for some reason he was unsuccessful with the part of the plan that had to do with my mother. It seems that the winds blew against the course of the ship, so to speak.

So my mother was prepared to go to Cairo and meet him there, to complete her life's journey with him wherever he went, or wherever they decided to be—in Cairo or in America. How was it that they made up with each other after she got married, and how were they able to contact each other? Directly or indirectly?

It's impossible that my mother did actually meet with Anwar after her marriage, not even once, for where could they have met? In Tripoli, the nearby city? She never went there by herself at all. She might have been able to meet him briefly once or twice in some place for a few minutes during which they managed to say a lot in a little bit of time. This might have happened, but I think they kept in touch through letters. No doubt, Anwar sent his letters to my mother through a friend of his who lived in New York. (Because most of the envelopes at my grandmother's house—my mother's mother's—had a New York postal stamp.) And that friend would send the letters to my mother at her parents' address. What made this little plan work was that my uncle—my mother's brother—who had emigrated to America, was living in New York, and wrote regularly to my grandparents. My mother was in charge of reading those letters, because both my grandparents were unable to read or write. So when a letter would arrive at my grandparents' house, and my mother would find out, she would rush over to open it and read it. My grandmother never touched those letters, because she considered them my mother's territory. And so did my grandfather, who was only interested in hearing what was in those letters once, or twice if there was something important. I bet that when my mother got a letter from Anwar she would read it as though it were from her brother, and she would improvise for her parents whatever came to mind or seemed plausible. And I'd also bet that when the need arose for her to read the letter a second time, she managed to do so without any problem.

Where did my mother hide all those letters? Did she burn them to make sure they didn't fall into the wrong hands? Did she memorize all that was in them? Did she memorize the addresses in Cairo, the phone numbers, in case some unexpected thing happened during her trip there and Anwar was not waiting for her at the airport or the seaport—as was the habit in those days—or in the train station, so she would know where to go?

My mother kept only the passport in her husband's house. Does she think it hasn't expired yet, and that the visa to Cairo is still valid? Is that why she kept the passport and the visa? She couldn't be that naive.

I think my mother kept all those letters in a special drawer in her parents' house. She would lock it up and put the key somewhere there. What made me believe this was that my grandmother would refer to that particular drawer as being "my mother's." She would say to me for example, "Put that thing on the dresser above your mother's drawer." Then, when her mother died, my mother burned all those letters. That was already long after her father passed away.

Several months after my grandmother died, the brothers and sisters divided the inheritance among them, and the house did not go to my mother. She confided in me that she no longer had a place in this whole world that she could call her own. I sympathized greatly with her, and I almost cried, my eyes welled up with tears, and I wanted to say to her, "My house will be a place for you to call your own." But the time was not ripe for risking such words.

Why didn't my mother go? What stopped her? I don't know. Did Anwar have to go to America for some reason, before she could have gone to Cairo? Did he meet another woman who made him forget my mother in the final stage of their plan? (Anwar remains a bachelor to this day.)

Did my mother go secretly to Beirut, with nothing but the clothes on her back—in order not to draw attention to herself with a suitcase—in order to board the boat to Cairo, but somehow got lost along the way? Did she get scared at the last minute of jumping into the unknown? Did she change her mind for some reason, and if so, what was the reason? I was definitely not the reason, because according to the date on the passport I was less than two years old at the time. In other words, I was right here on this earth when my mother decided she would run off secretly and leave me behind with my father and his family. It was not her great love for me or attachment to me that stopped her from taking such a great risk. Indeed it was a huge risk. First of all, she forged her husband's signature, and second, she wanted to *rendez-vous* with Anwar, which was even riskier, as far as my father was concerned, at least. In fact, the whole scheme, which she wove together perfectly, was a huge conspiracy the likes of which, as far as I know, had never been known in our conservative community before.

What my mother hoped to achieve through that complicated plan was to meet Anwar, the man she loved. But vengeance was her primary aim. Vengeance, definitely. Vengeance against my father, who she believed had degraded her, who was so harsh with her she couldn't bear it, the kind of harshness that no woman could bear, no matter how patient she was or how beaten down. My mother wanted to gain back her self-respect after suffering such unbearable degradation.

I was not the target. My mother did not want to abandon me because she hated me; rather, I was an unfortunate victim of circumstances. For the plan to work, there was no avoiding hurting me. Was my mother going to forget me for good, as if I never existed? And was she going to give birth to other children besides me, children she would care for out of pure love untainted by feelings of injustice—or something similar—that ate away at her?

"No one can walk in another person's shoes," my mother would say to Maryam from time to time. Was my mother burning inside to that extent? To the extent that she would weave together that intricate plot, thread by thread, in total secrecy, up until the very end, even until now? She did not tell anyone, not even Maryam, her closest and dearest friend.

I wonder what Maryam would have said about me if she had known what my mother was plotting. Would she have regarded me with more pity, pity perhaps bordering on contempt?

It really is strange that my mother kept Maryam in the dark about it. Was she afraid to tell her at first and then waited for a better time, but then decided not to tell her at all when there were clear signs that Maryam was going to marry her youngest brother-in-law? Or had she wanted to keep the secret safe so that she could always have the chance to take some far-off adventure whenever the time was right? It seems that this dream of hers was the right remedy for her anxiety, gloom, depression, and frustration. It was also a beautiful illusion she could not let go of; rather, she had to make sure not to let go of it and to safeguard it with every means in order to remain in control of her sanity.

Deep inside, my mother suffered a great deal, but she was responsible for this suffering, for part of it at least, since she was the one who gave my father the idea to seize the opportunity "Right now!"

It was my mother who set my father in motion. She made him ask for her hand with the urgency of "Right now!" Immediately, without waiting, and without wasting any time. I strongly believe the notion that a person brings problems upon oneself. Everyone does it somehow. I know this from Salwa in particular, because she brings the same kinds of problems upon herself over and over again and in almost the same way each time. She told me, for example, while complaining and being disgusted, that the concierge's son once wrote her a love letter. She always calls him the concierge's son, never by his name. He was twenty-five, ten years younger than she. Then later she said that he wrote her another letter, which she found "today" on her windshield tucked under the windshield wiper. She said, "I read it before I got into the car, then I looked around to see if he was still there watching me somewhere." I didn't say to her, "If you really didn't want him to write you a letter, you would have picked it up from the windshield as you would a dirty paper full of snot and spit and you would have thrown it on the ground without looking at it or him. Why on earth would you stand there on the road reading it except to make it clear that you had received it? You sent him a reply that goes like this: your letter has arrived and now all you need to do is wait to see my reaction, or make another one of your moves, if you can't wait." I didn't say this to her. Things like this always happen to Salwa. There are always admirers falling for her while she remains innocent and has nothing to do with their advances. No blame and no responsibility.

It was my mother who initiated my father's urgent request to marry her. My father realized, right away, that there was a major crisis underway between her and Anwar. He could see the worry in her eyes and her shaken self-confidence. So he talked to her as usual about general matters, and as usual he talked to her ready at any moment to move to more important matters, to the crux of the matter so to speak, as soon as she gave him a chance to do so. And my mother did give him the chance, and he took advantage of it immediately. The conversation developed quickly and took the direction that my mother wanted it to take—the one that would arouse Anwar's anger so much it would hurt—a pain he would never forget. My father said to her, "Whenever you want! Right away, if you want!"

"Right away!" my mother said.

In a moment of fury against Anwar, my mother aimed to destroy him without considering the dangerous consequences, the tragic consequences, that she would have to bear.

There's no question my mother thought she would always remain on top of anything that had to do with her and my father. She never imagined that the situation might turn on its head and that the same person who one day was waiting anxiously for a sign from her for a chance to fulfill her every desire, might tomorrow poison her life forever. Was it because she was so young that she behaved that way? And inexperienced? At that age a person has the impression that everything on earth will stay forever exactly as it is.

My mother never thought that my father would treat her in that violent, harsh, and hostile manner. She thought that the years of his tireless courtship, in which he used every trick in the book to attract her and convince her to marry him, meant she would always have power over him. She made an offhand calculation that all these efforts of his were good enough indication that he would never do anything to hurt her or upset her. And so she married him, in a fleeting moment of childish despair, amid a kind of tantrum. Just like that. *Sur un coup de tete!* He was waiting for her, as always, hoping for nothing more than for her to be pleased with him and accept him.

Why didn't my mother marry Anwar, the man she loved, and what happened to prevent her? She didn't talk much about that subject, but she did tell Maryam that she had informed him she was ready to go with him to America, where he was planning to go, and that they agreed to travel there after their marriage. So what was it that prevented it from happening? That is the fundamental question.

Apart from them themselves, there was no external reason that prevented them from marrying each other. My mother's family, I mean her father and her mother, would not have opposed the marriage, even if they had wanted to. And the same is true of Anwar's parents. And even if the families had objected, that would not have been an obstacle for them. Their personalities were much too strong for that. And so the actual reason had something to do with them themselves. So what was the reason?

My mother was a very proud woman. A lady. She would not accept being wronged. One of her character-istics was that she would break before she would bend. Especially since she was the type of person who thinks it is her God-given right that life be good to her and give her what she deserves. Did Anwar say to her jokingly, after she told him she was ready to go with him to America, "Who goes to a restaurant and brings his own food along with him?" Did that make her mad, so mad she decided to marry my father, who was accurately reading everything that was developing in her life? Had she been insulted by Anwar's joke?

Anwar always dreamed of traveling to America, and always by way of Egypt. My mother shared this dream, which seemed to be a constant topic of conversation between them. There's no doubt that talking about it developed into planning for it, in order to make it a real life experience. The agreement between them (or was it my mother's condition?) was that they get married here and then travel together. Did she sense that he was planning to go alone? Did she find out that he was trying to obtain a passport for him alone? Did she decide after that to set herself on fire so the flames would reach him and he would burn with her? Since she could not get what she wanted from him? Why is it that when my mother used to tell Maryam about this, she always seemed vague? Did he jokingly tell her something along the lines that it was futile to go with a woman to the United States, where women are free like men. Did he actually say that to her or not? And did he say it after she found out something that made her suspicious? Or did he say it before she discovered anything, which made her doubly attentive? My mother relates what Anwar said as if it were her own interpretation, nothing more. None of it did he actually say explicitly. There is no doubt that Anwar, with a statement like that, showed his reluctance, or gave away something he was hiding from my mother that had to do with my mother's travel to America with him. So did he make these kinds of statements often enough to instill doubt in my mother's heart?

My mother's ultimate goal was to have Anwar; reaching that goal would bring her total happiness. But she wanted him completely, from his inner depths, from the day he was born, and she was not ready to compromise on that. She was in love with him, but at the same time, she refused to be the only one who gave. She was in love with him to the utmost extent, and she was ready to go with him to the ends of the earth, but at the same time, she was not like a lot of women—she was not satisfied to be the fuel beneath her husband's flame. She wanted a relationship between two equals. And she was incapable of giving up what she considered herself worthy of, and what she considered her inalienable right, which did not depend on anybody's benevolence, compassion, or pity.

But my mother's fatal mistake was perhaps her belief, always and with insistence, that whatever she wanted must be, she must have, and that what she believed was rightfully hers she must obtain, and that whatever she deserved, she must also have.

I think her sense of justice and truth blinded her from the reality of this world, and for that she paid a high price and made others pay too.

But then there might have been something else that caused my mother to hotheadedly enter into marriage, out of anger, out of spite, and without considering the consequences. And also Anwar never openly admitted to my mother that he was the one who tossed the famous note to her while she was taking a bath at her parent's house when she was a young woman. And this is what she considered to be proof enough that, contrary to what she had hoped, she was not his first love nor his final goal, even though he had good times with her and was always happy to see her. (Just like me. Here I am, happy with Salwa and enjoying seeing her, without her being my final desire. Actually, I could drop her any time I want!) He would go along with her and humor her whenever she asked him if he was the one who tossed the note. He would dodge the issue. He would answer her with a question. He would say to her, for example, "And who could be the one who tossed it if it wasn't me?"

But I think the question that really went to the heart of the matter was why did my mother insist so strangely that it was Anwar who tossed her the note? Why? I can understand her wanting it to have been Anwar, I understand the desire and the wish, but for her to insist to that extent and to refuse to consider the facts, indeed to go so far as to fabricate facts and create a different truth— well, that is most strange.

All the bits of evidence I have come across and have managed to compile indicate that the note was not from Anwar, but rather from my father, which explains a lot of what happened later on. It might also explain why my mother threw herself at my father. But my mother ignored all these pieces of evidence and considered them trivial, useless. And she didn't like anyone to mention them at all. If anyone did, that is anyone like Maryam or, before her, my grandmother, she would get very angry.

My mother could not stand the presence of anybody who would disagree with what she maintained to be true concerning this subject.

I don't know why my mother insisted (and still insists) upon her opinion, despite the fact that everything contradicts that opinion. Why does my mother want Anwar to be the one who loved her from the very first moment, from the moment he discovered love? And why does she want so badly for him to be the one who tossed the note through the bathroom window, rather than my father or any other boy among her peers?

My mother always told the story of the note as if it were a love story suitable to be made into a movie. She would tell it as a beautiful love story, or the story of a beautiful love, and woe to anyone who would interrupt the flow of her storytelling! Woe to anyone who would get in the way of her love story, her life story.

My mother was fifteen years old and she was taking a bath. The bathroom had a little window overlooking the backyard. The time was one evening during school vacation. All of a sudden a small piece of paper came in through the window and landed on the floor. My mother was taken by surprise. She bent down to pick it up before it got wet. She picked it up and immediately tucked it under her clean clothes, which she had left on a chair in the corner of the bathroom. She continued her bath, more quickly now, and when she finished and got dressed, she opened the paper, a bit confused. It read: "I love you. Wear your yellow dress to school tomorrow."

My mother was thrilled by this beautiful surprise, the kind of thing she had always dreamed about. She hugged the note to her chest and closed her eyes like a movie actor would. My mother was born to be in the movies, body and soul. Born to be an actress or a producer or a script writer or something like that.

Whenever my mother reached this part of her story, she would act as if she were holding a precious treasure in her hand, which she hugged dearly to her chest while fluttering around in a circle.

Then suddenly my mother thought of the signature— she remembered she did not see any signature. She looked at the note again, but did not find a name. She turned it over and there was no name. There was nothing on the paper, not even a hint, about its author and sender. There was not a single clue. At any rate, the sender's identity did not concern her much, because she was convinced that she would find out soon enough. She was sure that it was one of those boys who she felt were always eyeing her, and especially Anwar who lately seemed to be practically eating her alive with his eyes. And it was his glances in particular that gave her the greatest excitement and joy. The thought of it being my father, Hamad, never even occurred to her, because he did not have to use such means to get to her. He could see her and talk to her whenever he wanted. He was her neighbor and her relative and he knew her house and everyone in it very well. He even knew what dresses she had and didn't have.

Hamad knew the color of every one of her dresses, which was an extremely simple matter because the number of dresses was fewer than the number of fingers on one hand.

Out of fear of it being discovered, my mother tossed the note into the toilet and flushed it. But before she did that, she read it again. She took a good look at it until its words were printed in her memory for ever, every detail of it. She wanted to get rid of it to make sure it didn't fall into her parents' hands, especially her mother's, who could not read and who would have sought the help of one or more neighbors who could read. In this way her private matter would have become the talk of the town. My mother then left the bathroom trying hard to control her nervousness so she wouldn't be discovered.

The next morning she did not wear her yellow dress. That was out of the question. *Et pour cause!* And for good reason!

My mother did not tell Maryam why she did not wear her yellow dress the next day, rather she did not admit to her the reason why, even though she did tell her she spent a long time getting ready, that she stood in front of the mirror for a long time and that she changed her clothes several times, so much that her mother noticed. Her mother said to her jokingly, "It's still early for this type of thing. Too early!"

And she answered, "Early for what?" pretending she didn't understand her mother's teasing.

When my mother left for school, her mother followed her to the door. She stood there watching her daughter as she walked toward school, something she rarely did. Then her father, who noticed his wife's unusual behavior, asked her what was going on.

"Our daughter is growing up!"

At that my mother nearly looked back in order to see with her own eyes what she had heard with her own ears. She did not expect her mother to be so aware of what was happening with her.

Is there anything better than this story, the way my mother tells it?

If only my mother were simply telling a good story. If only she were not interested at all in its being true or real, everything would have been as it should be. Everything would have been just right. Everything would have been fine and dandy! But.

But she told it as if it were absolutely true, exactly as she told it, forgetting there were some serious questions she could not answer if she were to keep her version of it and her interpretation of things.

For example, why didn't my mother tell Maryam the real reason she didn't wear a yellow dress, and why was it that when Maryam found out the real reason from my grandmother and confronted my mother with it, my mother became furious and denied it was true. She kept giving the same explanation, "Hamad knew our house very well. He would come and go as he pleased. He was our relative. Anwar, on the other hand, never set foot in our house even once."

She believed that this explained everything.

After the big fight that took place at school and which was undoubtedly caused by the note, my mother told her mother what happened, revealing everything, as if she were removing a heavy burden from her back. It seems she was afraid the situation would get worse. She knew that the reason for the fight at school had nothing to do with traditional family feuding, nor any other type of disagreement, but rather a falling out between Anwar and Hamad over her. This is the kind of reason that cannot be stated outright or proven, but is rather understood intuitively, or with something that resembles intuition. She did not, of course, tell her mother about what she was feeling inside and what she knew very well; she merely told her the story of the note.

My mother said that her mother's reaction was as follows:

"*I love you. Wear your yellow dress to school tomorrow.* What does that mean?" her mother asked, swept away by those words, which transported her to a different world altogether, a world she was not at all used to.

Then she added, "Is that it?"

"That's it," my mother said.

"Who wrote it?"

"I don't know! He didn't give his name or anything else!"

"And the note?"

"I flushed it down the toilet."

"Are you sure you read it correctly? We could have shown it to someone who can read well."

That was precisely what my mother had been afraid of, that her mother would show it to one of those "readers," most of whom were young and male. That was why she had gotten rid of it in the first place. But she always regretted she didn't keep it, if only to prove to Maryam that the handwriting was certainly not Hamad's.

"What is the world coming to!" her mother remarked disapprovingly.

After that her mother went into the bathroom, looked carefully for herself in every corner, hoping to find the note, even though the event had long passed. She looked at the little window from which the note came. She looked at it carefully and pondered. Then she dragged a chair beneath the window, stood on it, and strained to see through it to the outside, but didn't make any progress in the investigation.

The next day, the mother took her daughter to school. Her husband, surprised to see them leaving together, asked his wife, "Where to?"

"I'll be back."

Her answer infuriated him, but he only reacted by turning around quickly, going inside, and shouting at the top of his lungs, "What the hell!"

His response surprised my mother a great deal. She expected him to hit her mother or forbid her from going or at the very least force her to tell him where she was going.

She did not walk beside my mother, the way a mother and daughter might walk side by side as they went to the same destination. Instead she walked behind her, watching her from a distance. She watched her and everything around her (especially everything around her) out of the corner of her eye. And she was cursing the day she enrolled her daughter in that school. My mother had been attending the nuns' school, but then her father decided and her mother agreed to transfer her to a public school, which had started accepting girls. There was no reason to pay tuition to a private school, especially since she wasn't going to continue her studies no matter how well she did in school. My grandmother went into the school and headed straight to the administration office. She wanted to know the names of all the male students.

My mother tells this part of the story with notable innocence, I mean questionable innocence that raises doubts. She would tell it as if she didn't know that her mother was very worried, having immediately and perhaps instinctively made a connection between the note and the schoolyard fight, because there wasn't anyone who hadn't heard about it, and people talked about it for a long time. Rather the event was used as an excuse later on to support the opinion that there should be another school, thereby cutting down on the number of people (meaning the feuding families) occupying the same space. My grandmother went to the school because she was worried about this situation. She wanted to find out for herself what was going on and what the set-up was like. My grandmother was not at all comfortable with that story, so she went to the school.

"Who are the boys in my daughter's class?" She posed this question to the principal after finding out where his office was, much to the surprise of the students there who knew whose mother she was. The principal did not expect the question nor the urgency on the face of his unexpected visitor. She didn't give him a chance to welcome her, for example, or to say to her "Please come in." Or to suggest perhaps a cup of coffee, especially since he knew her and her husband well. And he knew all the stories of her family and their problems. Even though he was not from the town itself, he had been living there for some time, as the principal of one of its schools, and when he was appointed principal, all factions there accepted him as a person who was not under anyone's thumb, or for or against anyone.

Before answering her, he got up from his desk and closed the office door, after telling the teachers who had crowded around to find out what was going on to go back to their classrooms. He turned to her and said, "Has anyone misbehaved toward her? Has anyone bothered her?"

"No. No one bothered her. Her father wants to put his mind at ease."

Before pulling out her daughter's class roster, he asked her to have a seat. He offered her a cup of coffee or tea, but she thanked him and apologized that she had to get back home right away and didn't have time to sit.

The principal read off the names of all the boys in her daughter's class. (Anwar's name and the name of my father Hamad were among them.) Then he read off the names of the boys in the next class down. There wasn't any name in particular that attracted her attention. (This is what my mother says, or alleges!) So she became even more confused, which was very obvious to the principal, who in turn became worried. He, especially, knew how sensitive the situation at the school was with a school body from all the various families in town. Hardly a few months had passed since the clash between the students belonging to my mother's family (that is the family of Hamad my father) and the students from Anwar's family, in which they pounded each other with their fists hard enough to kill each other. The one would strike the other with all his might, his anger, and his fear, in order to kill him if he could. This scene terrified the principal, since that was the first time he had ever seen a student hit another student intending to kill him. The schoolyard turned into a huge arena with the fighters at the center surrounded by excited onlookers. The principal, the assistant principal, and some teachers tried to interfere at first, but they soon realized that they were only exposing themselves to real danger. They backed off, not knowing what to do. But the principal realized right away that the situation was serious enough to call for the police to come and break up the fight and to shift the responsibility away from himself and the teachers, especially since the events might develop and someone might get hurt, something which was outside the school's jurisdiction. Just before the police arrived the students stopped fighting. They had been warned by other students that the police were coming. But no one could hide what had transpired, especially since the police, who knew very well the extent of the hostilities among those families, and in order to save face, insisted that those "responsible" be turned over to them. Two students from each side were turned in, but the negotiations between the police, the principal, and the students went back and forth and on and on. The principal denied that he knew who started it or caused it, and the students hid behind their silence and denied that they saw who was the cause and who started it. The police did not want to apprehend everyone who was involved in the fight, first because there were too many of them, and second because the police couldn't bear the responsibility for such a decision. As for the students who were turned in, they were too young and were not involved in the fight at the same level as the older students. The police were more than happy to have them as a way out of the crisis. So they took them away in the police car, set them free after a short time, and handed them over to some women not their mothers, as their mothers were not called to the police station for fear they would run into each other and the situation would get worse. My grandmother, my mother's mother, was the one who went to pick up my father Hamad's youngest brother.

Anwar was among the fighters and so was Hamad. In fact, the whole fight started with them. They swung at each other without mercy.

The principal asked my grandmother again if anything had happened to her daughter to disturb her. Again she said no, and assured him that the whole matter was that her father simply wanted to put his mind at ease concerning his daughter.

"You know how things are around here!"

"Yes, of course," the principal said, unconvinced.

My grandmother stood a short distance from the gate as the children were being dismissed from school. She scrutinized each one of the boys as they passed by, but she was unable to settle on any one in particular. She went home demoralized, walking quickly behind her daughter, who had just left school and hadn't noticed her mother.

My mother did not tell her friend Maryam that her mother, my grandmother, said that she suspected Hamad. But she admitted it to her, after Maryam confronted her one day with what my grandmother had already told her. My grandmother said to Maryam that she suspected Hamad was the one who sent the note, and she said she was very surprised when the principal read Hamad's name off the class list.

"Hamad is in her class!" she said with uncontainable shock (that did not strike her when Anwar's name was read.)

The principal was surprised she didn't know that Hamad was in her daughter's class, and was also surprised by her reaction. But my grandmother pretended that everything was normal and there was nothing for her to be surprised or bewildered about. But later she confided to Maryam that her heart had been set on fire! She knew that Hamad was cruel and violent, and she knew that he liked her daughter. She could tell by the way he looked at her when he came to the house and from the kind of apprehensive questions he would ask when she wasn't home, in spite of giving the impression that he was not asking about her for any particular reason. My grandmother had seen him when she went to the school to find out what was going on and what the set-up was like.

"When I saw Hamad, he avoided me and didn't talk to me, as if he was embarrassed. Sometimes I think he is the one!"

My mother was furious when her mother told her all these actions she had undertaken. "Why is this matter so important to you?" my mother asked disapprovingly. "This is my business, and my business alone!"

Her mother shook her head and didn't say a word.

"And what has Hamad got to do with all this?" my mother added.

That was precisely what was hurting my mother and making her upset. In her opinion, Hamad should be left out of the matter completely, and should not be brought into something he had nothing to do with.

"Hamad has his eyes on you," her mother said. "I see his admiration in the way he looks at you. He wants you, I can tell, but it seems that you have your eyes on someone else."

"I know who it was!" my mother interrupted, putting a stop to her mother's account of things.

"Then who was it?" her mother asked.

"Anwar!" my mother said.

My grandmother was completely silent and did not show any reaction whatsoever, as if she hadn't heard a thing.

Then after that, as the saying goes, "the party was over and it was time to sober up." In other words, my mother had awakened from her dream and realized that she was living her desires as if they were reality, and that this, unfortunately, could not go on forever. And where, indeed, was that yellow dress the author of the note wanted her to wear?

"The party is over and it's time to sober up." She removed every piece of clothing from her closet, but there was no yellow dress.

Quite simply, my mother did not own a yellow dress.

No matter how stubbornly my mother tried to stretch things to the limit, she simply could not change the names of colors. It seems she did have a dress that was yellowish, but could never really be called *yellow*. The only piece of truly yellow clothing she had was a yellow wool sweater. There was no doubt about its yellowness, but it was a sweater, and what had been requested in writing was a dress. Besides, it wasn't winter time, nor was it cold.

Her face flushed as she frantically searched her closet. Sweat beaded on her upper lip, on both sides (sweat always appears there first on my mother). Then she bit her lower lip with her upper teeth and her eyes welled with tears.

"Why?"

Was there some mistake, and what was it?

Her mother came in and saw my mother in that state, sitting in front of the empty closet with all her clothes strewn about the room, and gasped. She hesitated for a moment and then said without introduction, "Tomorrow you'll have a yellow dress."

"But he wants to see *my* yellow dress!"

"What do you mean? Isn't a dress you buy with your father's hard-earned money yours?" Her mother said that, quite upset.

My mother rushed to the bathroom and locked the door behind her with the key. She looked down into the toilet and examined every bit of it. Then she stood on a chair and looked out the window with despairing eyes. Then she went back and found her mother where she had left her. She approached her and asked her, pointing to the dress that bordered on yellowness, "Mom. Isn't this dress yellow?"

My grandmother always said that my mother was very stubborn. She would say about her, "You're right, it's yellow, even if it can fly," alluding to the saying, "You're right, it's a goat, even if it can fly." She said that to her in front of me once while they were arguing with each other about my father, a constant point of contention between them. My grandmother always urged my mother to focus her efforts and her mind on her house and not waste her time crying over the past.

My mother stopped secretly examining the boys as she had done in the past and started instead to watch the girls and see what color clothes they wore. In her heart she knew which one of her girlfriends had a yellow dress. Definitely yellow. Pure yellow. Yellow yellow. (But the note had been sent to *her*, thrown through *her* bathroom window.) She was overcome with colors. She no longer saw anything but colors, colors of all colors. In the past, she would look at the style, but now it was the color. She used to look at the cut, but now it was the color. She used to look at whether it was fashionable or not fashionable, pretty or ugly, current or passé, but now it was the color. The color and nothing else. At school she noticed the color of the chalkboard and the color of the chalk; she noticed the color of the teacher's fingers, the color of his finger-nails, and saw the difference between them and the difference between the color of the face and the hands and the color under the fingernails. And she noticed the hair color of every student sitting in front of her, and saw that there were different shades of black, and that they were only called black by convention. And yellow was the same way. There wasn't just one color yellow. There was actually a wide spectrum of colors one could call "yellow."

She said to her friend, as they were walking to school, that she dreamed often of buying new clothes.

"Did you win the lottery or something?" her friend answered and then asked her why she was so distracted these days.

In class she concocted a handwriting contest. "Who has the nicest handwriting?" she asked the student sitting next to her, loud enough for everyone to hear.

The students congregated around her desk, and each one wrote a phrase on her notebook and signed his name underneath. Hamad and Anwar were among those students who did not participate in the contest.

When she got home, my mother opened up her notebook and looked over the various handwritings, trying to remember if one of them was the same as the handwriting on the note. Then she took her notebook with her and went to the bathroom to look for the note which she had intentionally thrown away, regretting that she did throw it away. She gazed at the spot where she threw it and then she looked all around the bathroom hoping to somehow find it somewhere.

If only she could tell her teacher about what was boiling inside her heart! If only she could ask him to ask the students who wrote a note and tossed it to her.

If only.

For sure the teacher could help her more than any other person. And definitely more than her mother.

My mother went through a very difficult period of weakness and doubt, but it was also during that time that her relationship with Anwar was established. She started meeting him secretly and surely asked him about the note. He answered with what might be taken to mean yes. In other words, that he was the one who wrote the note, but sent someone else to deliver it. The answer satisfied my mother who was head over heels in love and happiness over their relationship. She thought that the very fact they got together was ample proof that he was the one who tossed the note, especially since no one else had come forward after that except for him! In addition, he really liked the way she looked in yellow clothes, which for his sake she started buying in quantity. "You look best in yellow," he always said to her, especially in the first stage of their relationship. The relationship lasted that way for three years. They met most of the time in the photography studio he opened and worked in, selling everything that had to do with movies and famous movie stars. It was an ideal place for a young man and a young woman to meet, at that time in particular, when it was difficult for young men and young women to be alone together. And that was why it was possible for their relationship to go as far as it did.

But Maryam, despite her love for my mother and their strong friendship, always posed questions that cast doubt on my mother's story. In particular, the part about which one of them—Anwar or Hamad—sent the note.

It seems that Maryam was more taken by my mother's personality, vivacity, and boldness, than she was convinced by her logic. My mother's problems fascinated her. She loved stories of the heart and its torment. She would identify with the lovers and always dream of falling in love herself. That's what she always expressed to my mother, who advised her never to get married without being in love. Then Maryam would answer that she was getting on in years, that she was becoming more and more worried about the future, and could not afford to be fussy any longer.

As far as Maryam was concerned, my mother's stories were love stories she loved to hear.

My mother was truthful about everything and only resorted to hiding the truth when it came to particular subjects: the identity of the author of the note, and her planned trip to Cairo to meet Anwar. Everything else, however, she told with embarrassing frankness, with deadly frankness.

And if my mother kept Maryam in the dark about Hamad and the note because of her desire to fashion a new reality, she was dying of an even greater desire to reveal to her the story of her planned trip to meet Anwar in Cairo and cherish every word of it.

I'm sure of one thing: my mother did not tell Maryam about her secret plan to travel to Cairo because, as I've always thought, she was at first afraid of revealing it, simply afraid. Later, she was waiting for just the right moment to tell her, but then something happened to change her mind, not intentionally at first. What happened might have been hints about the possibility of opening channels of dialogue with her youngest brother-in-law. It was as though very early on she picked up the scent of a relationship being cooked up, over a slow flame, between Maryam and my youngest uncle, one of the boys who had been turned in to the police after the schoolyard incident that followed the tossing of the note. The ones responsible for "cooking up" this relationship were their parents and relatives, without the knowledge of Maryam at first, and definitely against her wishes. Actually, Maryam did not like him, but with the passing of days, years rather, she started saying to herself, "why not?"

And she started thinking that she could accept him as a husband who could "protect" her. There was no love between them. From her point of view at least, it was strictly speaking a rational marriage, a wise decision.

I've always said that it was that same youngest uncle who was sent by my father to toss the note to my mother. And I've always said that my father certainly did not permit him to read the note, and did not tell him anything about its contents, neither then or afterward. I say this out of a deep-seated feeling I have, although I have no way to prove it. My father chose him to undertake this mission because a young boy would not attract attention if he were to jump up and toss something through a bathroom window.

And it so happened that Maryam did marry that youngest uncle of mine. My mother was truly a woman with foresight and sharp intelligence.

My father adored this uncle most of all. It is well known that in our society the eldest brother has a special kind of love for his youngest brother. But my father did not show in any way whether he was pleased with the idea of this marriage or not. He stayed out of it. I mean, he let things happen without opposing them and without having any influence on them, neither positively nor negatively. He knew, of course, about the strong friendship between Maryam and my mother, and he felt Maryam was afraid of him in a way, or was intimidated by him, or seemed to be on her guard in his presence, most likely because of what he imagined my mother told her about him. So did that mean he was against the marriage? Or did that close friendship between my mother and Maryam make him favor supporting the marriage in order to separate them? In other words, to keep Maryam busy with a life of her own, busy enough at least to stop her daily visits to my mother.

My mother, on the other hand, openly showed her support for the marriage, without hesitation and with a frankness that does not admit of doubt. Yet what she actually felt deep inside her was a secret that could easily be fathomed. My gut feeling is that deep inside she did not wish for Maryam to marry my uncle. She had hoped that Maryam would marry someone who would keep her nearby, and her marriage to my mother's brother-in-law would not fulfill this hope. She kept all these feelings inside, and never allowed them to show. For Maryam's wedding gift, my mother gave her a refrigerator, and such a present in those days was substantial. The kind of gift a very wealthy person would give. She paid for it with her own money, which she received from time to time as her share of the income from her parents' land earnings, or from the money her brother in America sent to her. My father never asked her about this money.

Maryam remained good friends with my mother after she got married, but naturally she was no longer able to spend all her time with her as she did when she was single.

And my mother also kept that friendship going as much as she could. She visited Maryam in her new home (her husband's house) several times, both when my youngest uncle (her husband) was at home and when he was not at home. My uncle welcomed my mother and treated her cordially (nothing more than that!) and he would leave them alone in the house, or in whichever room they were in, to give them a chance to talk freely. That was his way of showing respect for his wife, and showing his desire to call a truce with my mother, or to make amends and forget the past. (When I think of it now, that was one thing that made me very happy and removed the thorns of doubt that pierced my heart.) My mother also showed her desire to call a truce and reciprocated each step he took with one of her own. It was out of great foresight on her part that she prepared the way and allowed for that to happen by saying to Maryam, when she saw that matters were heading down a one-way road to marriage, "You're doing the right thing. A marriage based on mutual agreement has many advantages." She told Maryam that she was sure my uncle loved her, that she would be able to get along with him, and that he would not necessarily behave as my father did. Once, before they were married, my mother invited them along with some other neighbors to her house for coffee. My father was not there. During that visit my mother was extremely nice, not only to the guests, but to me as well. And my uncle was very friendly, too, not only to my mother, but to me, too. Those were unusual moments. He took out an expensive fountain pen from his pocket. It was gold-plated. He handed it to me and said, "God willing, you will use this to earn the highest degrees!" I took it from him with deep joy, great joy, intoxicating joy. I tried, however, not to allow these feelings, with all their intensity, to surface. I did not want my uncle or anyone else to make connections between things. I did not want the heat of the moment to conjure up the coldness of the past, and its frigidity (and its poisons). I kept the pen in my hand throughout the visit, the token of a historic pact.

My mother continued to feel that Maryam was on her side and supportive of her for a very long time. She kept on telling her every bit of new news or continued retelling the old stories and their impact on her life. In her turn, Maryam shared with my mother her relationship with her husband, telling her details about things that were not easy to reveal. At that stage I had become a young man, but they did not hold back from discussing in front of me these personal female matters. It was as though Maryam wanted to make me forget that I had come of age, and as though by persisting to act the same as always around my mother she wanted to say to me that what took place between us that one day was a dream that I alone dreamed. Naturally I did not sit by them as I did when I was a child, but I was always there, either passing by or busy with something, though my presence never bothered them. Often I would eavesdrop. Maryam told my mother that on their first night together after the wedding, my uncle got off of her, after he made her bleed, put on his clothes, and went out. He came back quickly to tell her that he couldn't go out, because everyone who saw him would ask him why. That was his first night with his bride, and on that particular night the groom is never seen at any other place. Deep in her heart she was sad when he returned, because she wanted to sleep, and she was afraid he would come back at her a second time. And indeed that was what happened. He tried a second time before the blood had stopped flowing. He hurt her even more than the first time. She also told my mother that she did not enjoy herself at all—he panted and snorted like a wild animal, to the point that she was afraid there might be something wrong with him. She would say to herself, "What a disaster! What if something happens to him? What will I do?" She conceived two children by him—a boy and a girl. She continues to ask my mother about real pleasure, the orgasm that shakes your whole body and sends you soaring to seventh heaven.

One day she told my mother something very serious, which worried my mother a great deal. She told my mother that he asked her about their relationship, that is,

Maryam's relationship with my mother. "What do you think? She's my closest friend," she responded. In fact my mother was expecting him to ask such a question. She was sure that he would ask her sooner or later, and she wanted many times to ask and nearly did ask Maryam if her husband was asking about their relationship and whether he wanted Maryam to tell him some of her news—my mother's news. (Did my mother want to ask Maryam if he had told her he was the one his brother Hamad sent to deliver the note?) My mother didn't dare ask the question, and instead waited for the right time. She was certain the right time would come. It was just a matter of waiting. She knew Maryam was a real friend, and she knew that she loved her and would not keep from her anything that happened between her and her husband, especially if that particular thing involved her. And that precisely was the case. One day my uncle asked his wife Maryam about my mother's relationship with Anwar. He asked her if my mother had told her Anwar was the one she lost her virginity to, and when.

(And when? My God, his interest in determining the specific time concerns me directly! In other words, the question is about me! Oh God! Oh God! Oh uncle! All those things are still alive in your heart!)

He actually said to her that he and his brothers were sure of that—that Anwar was the one she lost her virginity to and not their eldest brother. He also said that although these matters had been forgotten they were still present in their hearts and souls.

(Forgotten!)

My uncle did not tell Maryam if my uncles had one day planned to kill my mother. (They did want to, and I am so sure of that I won't even discuss it with anyone. But did they actually plan it out one day?) Maryam had no knowledge of any of that, neither did she know anything about my cousin's wife whom my uncle got rid of after his son—her husband—was killed, but she had every reason to have her doubts about the matter. Nor did my mother know anything about the subject, except that the young bride, who had only been married a few short months, disappeared after going crazy over the murder of her beloved husband. My mother did have many reasons, however, to wonder about it quietly, deliberately, and carefully. (Every mad man has a rope to hang himself with—as the men in our family say.) Only the men had knowledge of that incident. Only the brothers and anyone else who can get information somehow or who can read that which has been erased, or who has the ability decipher secret codes. Only other male relatives who were obligated not to talk because revealing any of it would mean betrayal and consequently, assassination. To even contemplate whether or not it really happened was completely for-bidden. And even to know the truth had a sort of ambiguous nature. This total ban was highly respected as a divine law that could not be discussed, could not even be thought about.

My mother's and Maryam's friendship remained strong for many years after Maryam's marriage, but life has a way of forcing people apart with its daily chores and responsibilities that seem to have no end but rather keep increasing every day. The children grow as do the worries. This is what parents always say as a way of apologizing for not being able to accept some invitation.

My mother and Maryam were able to preserve their old friendship, their love, and their constant desire to visit each other whenever possible. They remained *complices* throughout all those years that followed Maryam's marriage.

But the schism finally came. A schism brought on by a massive earthquake—the murder of Maryam's sixteen-year-old son.

I believe that incident put Maryam in a position in which she could not avoid revealing things about my mother (meaning me, too!) that no one should know, especially since the murderer was one of Anwar's relatives, or in other words from the side Anwar belonged to by nature and birth. At the time, Anwar had long since moved to the United States.

Is it possible that my uncles were not aware of every detail concerning me and my mother? Is it possible that they did not inform my father?

(Was my father still lacking information about that relationship? Didn't he know everything? The central question and all its details? There was no doubt that what he knew was more than enough, and he was satisfied with it.)

Maryam's son, my cousin, the first born of his parents, was in his first year of high school. He had started reading books that were not part of his school curriculum, books that were concerned with "social matters," meaning in a broad sense "politics." Not politics in its restricted sense of elections, but in the more general meaning of change. Little by little, this young man started considering himself above the blood feuds among the families in the town, and so he started going deliberately to places where a whole lot of different people congregated. In fact, he started going to areas usually off limits to him. One time he was caught there. He did not sense the coming danger and underestimated the seriousness of what was being devised at that stage, and so he was killed. Sixteen years, just like that, dumped on the side of the road, in broad daylight. His mother Maryam went crazy when she received the phone call.

When the telephone rang, Maryam was home alone. Her only daughter was outside, and so was her husband. She could not identify the voice of the caller who said, "So you'll understand how valuable children are!"

Then he hung up without saying who he was or explaining what he meant by that poisonous phrase. Maryam's heart was on fire. She knew what side he was on if not who he was exactly. She called for the neighbors and the relatives and contacted the network of people who were always the first to get news, until she understood fully the meaning of the phrase. She collapsed saying, "My son!"

She no longer had a son. She had only her twelve-year-old daughter. Maryam did not want many children because she had difficulty in childbirth and she wanted her two children to live comfortably and have everything they needed. Maryam couldn't bear to see a needy child, and in her eyes, having a child one could not afford to raise was a sin.

Then Maryam sent for her husband to come right away. She was insistent that he should come to her, which bewildered the relatives and the neighbors who had come to her house as soon as they heard the news. They were bewildered by her insistence, for what could her husband do now? What happened happened. And besides, men mourn with other men in such circumstances, not with women around. But she kept on insisting until her husband arrived. She pulled him to a wall with her back to it, lifted her skirt with one hand all the way up to her waist, and with the other hand she pulled him toward her and screamed, "Give me a baby! Give me a baby right now! I want a baby now! If we don't have a son, they will humiliate us, they will destroy us!"

But her husband hit her hard on the hand that was lifting the skirt and pulled her into an empty room. "Your son was murdered!" he screamed at her.

Maryam changed a lot after her son was murdered. She wrapped herself in black mourning clothes and did not give them up for a long time. When she finally did stop wearing those black clothes, she continued to mourn deep inside her heart and soul. My mother, especially during the first period after Maryam's son died, never left her alone, as if she were on one long never-ending visit to console her, make her forget, and convince her that she should have a new child and that she should consult a doctor if she was having any problems conceiving. "A child now will keep you company and cheer you up and make up for some of your loss," my mother said to her. Maryam was always happy to have my mother around, but she no longer asked my mother how she was doing, about her problems, or about the story of the old love affair that had occupied her dreams for years and even decades. Part of the reason was that whenever my mother came to visit, there were many other visitors around—relatives and neighbors. And Maryam no longer visited my mother at all. The reason at first was related to the incident and the deep wounds it inflicted, wounds that were always festering and never healing. Then things changed and kept on changing until the routine took a different form. In fact Maryam's whole disposition changed and her concerns changed. She was very worried about her husband and would wait impatiently for him to come home each day, which was quite different from the way, as she confided to my mother, she used to care less if he came home or went out. She did get pregnant once, less than two years after her son was murdered, but she was unable to hold on to the fetus and had a miscarriage in the third month.

But not one bad word about my mother ever left Maryam's tongue.

After Maryam, my mother never had another friend.

In principle, they remained friends, but after a while they had nothing to talk about and did not get together. This situation only made my mother more bitter. She was all alone and entered into a state of loneliness she couldn't get out of. She was no longer able to build a new friendship, and her feeling of bitterness increased with time. It became more and more difficult for her to live on the brighter side of life, and that was reflected in her relationship with me more than in her relationship with my father. With my father, her behavior was set from the very first years of her marriage, rather the first few weeks. She knew her limits. What she could and couldn't do. From the very first year of their marriage she would go to the store to buy everything she needed for the house and my father would pay the grocer directly at the end of each month. As for the other expenditures that were not directly related to the house, my mother paid for those from her own savings. My father never discussed financial matters with her. On the other hand, her relationship with me was not subject to the same strict rules. It varied and changed according to the mood and the circumstances. I mean, my mother would never shout at my father no matter what. She would never even raise her voice to him. That wasn't the case with me. She screamed at me whenever she wished or whenever she felt it was necessary to do so. Some of her feelings toward me, however, were constant and unchanging. I used to feel inside that she was making fun of me, that she didn't have the kind of feeling toward me that mothers have toward their children. Whenever I succeeded at something—a diploma or a job—she would act as though it was a common occurrence, no big deal. When I passed the Baccalaureate, which was extremely difficult in those days, she received the news with conspicuous indifference. She smiled a little, blushed a little, and the neighbors came to congratulate her. She received them politely enough, while one of our neighbors bought a box of chocolates and offered them to passersby in celebration as she had done the year before when her own son passed the Baccalaureate.

From the time I was a small child, that is, since I became aware of myself and what was around me, my mother treated me in a surprising manner. I mean ever since I became conscious of things, I would notice that my mother was treating me in a strange way. She did not treat me the same way my friends' mothers treated my friends. This was a strange feeling. And it becomes even stranger when I say it and acknowledge it, even if only to myself. Because I didn't live it in those precise words. For example, I always felt kind of bothered when Maryam would discuss those extremely personal things in front of me. And this feeling got worse as I grew older. What bothered me most was how boldly she talked with my mother about things most people would have difficulty discussing in front of someone else. Maryam would talk to her in front of me about whatever she pleased with no caution or shame. Strange how parents can be ignorant of such important matters! Those things leave a lasting impression on their children. Stories that can crush their self-esteem and attack the very heart of their identity and sense of belonging! Do they, I mean parents, actually forget that children can hear and see and understand? Or maybe she wanted, intentionally or not intentionally, to hurt me for life because I was the undesired fruit of her womb. (This actually was what made me very happy throughout my youth. Yes, it made me very happy to be the undesired fruit of her womb. I emphasize "undesired.") I often felt that my mother was taking things out on me, vengeance for some pain she suffered on account of me. This feeling of mine increased as I grew older, especially in most recent years, perhaps because my visits to her have become less and less frequent. It is strange how in recent years she has become even more nervous and intent upon hurting me. The last time I visited her before my father was murdered, I mean when I visited them a few months before my father was murdered, I brought my book for learning English with me so I could continue practicing and reviewing and not forget what I had been learning, and to do a few more lessons during those few days. At this age, my problem with learning English is that I forget things. I don't have a problem with comprehension. I comprehend very quickly, but I soon forget what I've just learned. This is why learning English has become a kind of obsession for me. The obsession goes beyond learning English into much deeper psychological issues, as if it were connected to my advancing years. That is, conquering this forgetfulness has become a challenge and a measure of my mental vitality. I decided I would learn in one go, without stopping. That would be better than dragging it out forever, especially since learning English has become a must for anyone who wants to live in this age without feeling alienated and left out. I was in a mental state that would not allow me to leave my book behind during my visit to my parents, even though I knew by intuition, if not from experience, that my mother would use that book as an opportunity to humiliate me. Yes, to humiliate me and scoff at me. My father, however, was not interested in such matters. He wouldn't even notice, and even if he did, he wouldn't give any of it a second thought. The house and everything in it was extraneous to his real life. His real life was outside, outside the house, taking care of his olive and lemon groves, which provided a small income, and mediating every transaction that had to do with the buying and selling of real estate, cars, and anything else that can be bought or sold. My father also intervened to solve problems over loan debts. There are many people who borrow money and put up a piece of land or a house or something like that as collateral, and when the loans come due, they are unable to pay for some reason or other, which leads to disagreements between the parties, and these disagreements sometimes escalate. My father would intervene and help the parties come to an agreement, receiving in return some money, the amount of which depended on the particular people involved, or the seriousness of the disagreement, or the degree to which they wanted to seek favor with my father's family. Sometimes my father would lend money also, but only if the borrower was a decent person and not a troublemaker, and only if he had enough securities to guarantee payment when the time came. That was because my father did not like to get caught up in problems over debts. He was always ashamed of the behavior of some tyrannical lenders, as he described them, who sometimes, when debts were not paid on time, would go so far as to shove the person who owed money, if he had no one to defend him, into the trunk of a car, right in the middle of the square for everyone to see and then take him to his house where they would open the trunk in front of his wife and children, boys and girls alike. The debtor would get out from the trunk drowning in sweat and silence. The second time around they would pay him a visit at his house when he wasn't home, and they would discuss the problem and the possible solutions with his wife or his eldest daughter, showing total flexibility and willingness to find a solution that did not lack in generosity. My father really hated this. He hated money lending. He considered it a kind of sin, but sometimes, and only sometimes, some person would come to him who really needed some money immediately, and he couldn't turn him down. Most of the time he would say no, even in such urgent cases.

And so it was that under the heavy pressure I had put upon myself, I took with me the book I was using to learn English and its accompanying cassette tape. Several hours after I arrived, and after I made the usual rounds among friends and acquaintances in the places where they congregate and socialize, I returned to the house. My mother was sitting in the living room, or what we have come to call the TV room, watching an American film. That to her was the nicest thing on earth—watching an American film in the evening. For her, it was opium that washed away all the worries of the world, and the worries of the day and of the night. Like many of the educated people of my generation, I would not watch such a film, since it did not live up to my cultural standards. So I decided to take advantage of what was left of the evening to review a lesson in my English book. I put the tape into the tape player in the parlor, and I opened the book, listening and repeating after the lesson on the tape. That was my particular way of learning—listen to the tape first and recognize every single word and letter, and then read it from the book.

This is why I always had to replay the tape, in order to hear the same phrase and sometimes the same word several times to make sure I really knew it before I read it. That was my philosophy for learning languages. My purpose was to understand the spoken before the written. I imagined and dreamed that I would soon meet a lot of people and I would be able to communicate with them; I would meet people I knew only by name, liked very much, and whose opinions I appreciated. People I considered to belong to the same space as I, the same time, the same *territoire*, the same values. I have always believed (and I still do) that we should discuss the nature of this space. (And this is what is referred to in the current nationalistic terminology as the homeland, the national soil, within the borders, et cetera.) And we should discuss all the issues related to this space, especially now that the Internet has become widespread and has developed rapidly and holds so much promise. I remain certain that there are a lot of people who belong to this same *territoire*, and what binds them sometimes is much more important than what binds two neighbors or two people from the same nation or homeland or sect or religion, who happen to be neighbors or members of the same nation or homeland, and so on. Which is why I am learning English, because it is at present the available means for achieving this goal, and not necessarily out of love for the language, or out of admiration for any special merits it has over other languages, and not necessarily out of dislike of another language or to belittle its importance. The truth is, today English is *the* language, so why not use it as a means of uniting people, bringing them closer, helping them to know each other (and hate each other!) without any national or cultural fanaticism or other such things. Just like that. Especially since there is a huge interactive relationship between English (and the other western languages, especially French) and Arabic. All one has to do is read *Time* or *Newsweek*, for example, (from time to time, with the patience of Job, I used to read short passages from them) to realize that in a way one is reading Arabic. There are many expressions that are common to the two languages, and more than being mere expressions, they are symbols that define the thought process. Rather they are modes of thought.

By the way; on the other hand; without doubt; burning question; sooner or later; at least; keep an eye on; on the brink of collapse; fearing the worst; killing... and injuring; just in time; in fact; more than ever; short-sightedness; in big part; this puts Airbus almost on an equal footing with Boeing; what is required; work hand in hand; in addition to; taken into account; according to; from time to time.

And so many other expressions that make you feel when reading them that you are reading Arabic in English, and which make it easy for you to understand and promises you quick progress in the language.

I was replaying the tape to hear an especially difficult expression, an expression that was impossible for me. (What makes learning this language especially difficult for me is my hearing. I have problems hearing, hearing certain letters in particular, such as the "s" or the "th" in "the" and the "f" or the "th" in "thin" and so on. This makes following my particular method for learning, which basically relies on listening, a difficult thing indeed. So difficult sometimes it's impossible. My father did not suffer at all from these problems. He had the ears of a mole! God! It's amazing how the embers are always hiding under their own ashes!)

And so as I was replaying that difficult expression that was impossible for me, no matter how many times I replayed it, because of those letters I had difficulty with, I turned the volume way up and put my ear right up against the speaker, listening with full attention over and over again. And just as I was in the middle of that my mother opened the door, and gave me a most bewildered look. So I turned the volume down and smiled at her like a small child who had gotten caught doing something wrong. I tried to say something, but words betrayed me. So she spoke first with biting sarcasm.

"*Do you speak English?*"

"*How are you?*"

She burst out laughing as she repeated these two phrases again and again, dancing around in circles, until she was bent over as if someone had punched her in the stomach. She leaned against the first sofa she could find in order not to fall down. Then she looked at me as if I had reminded her of something deep and distant. She was looking at me without actually seeing me. Through me she was pondering something in her own soul. Then she came to, all of a sudden, and went back to the TV to watch the rest of her movie, with the tranquility of someone who has been given a shot of morphine that has just taken effect.

My mother was wearing her *robe de chambre*. It was sky blue. I'll never forget that. It was long and almost touched the floor and accentuated her beautiful figure. My mother is a beautiful woman.

What could I say? I was confused and embarrassed. I wished the earth would split open and swallow me into its belly. I wished I had never made this damned visit.

The older I get the more I believe in this theory of mine. People bring problems upon themselves! What happened to me there was one more proof. I expected that kind of sarcastic response from my mother, so why did I set everything up for her? I had expected that kind of response, especially since she had given me fair warning a few years back.

"What's that?" she asked me the first time she saw me immersed in a book for learning English. She smiled when I answered her that I wanted to learn English. Then she said sarcastically, trying to hold back her laughter. "*How are you?*" I was embarrassed and wanted to hide the book, but I was afraid I would be making it worse for myself, so I tried to appear preoccupied with my book, but I couldn't. So I hoped to diffuse the enormous nervousness that took hold of me, but couldn't think of anything except to cry. I didn't cry, though. I wasn't capable of crying.

I was expecting that kind of reaction from my mother, but not with such meanness, because I thought that she had gotten used to the idea that I was learning English and that her reaction, in case it came up, would be a faint smile, or a hand gesture suggesting she couldn't be bothered, all to say that I was still the same and I hadn't changed. But I did not expect that horrible explosion. Why was my mother still intent on hurting me? Why? In fact it seemed her desire to hurt me increased as she got older. One would have expected the years to have softened her. Was it because I had distanced myself from her, stopped visiting her as often? Was it because I rarely called her on the phone to ask how she was doing and feeling and to ask my customary question about my father, which she always used as an excuse to say: "Your father is a bachelor looking for a bride!" Was it because this distancing on my part released her negative feelings toward me, causing her to want to hurt me more as a result, to the point—and she being the lady that she is— to the point that she started overlooking good table manners in my presence? She would stick her finger into her mouth while we were eating, for example, to pick out pieces of food that were stuck in her teeth. Then she would wipe her fingers on bread that she would later put back in the bread bag with the smeared food particles still on it. She would then put out the same piece of bread on the table at the next meal.

This despite the fact that my mother was very particular about manners in general, and she brought me up that way.

I claimed during one of my last visits that I was going to the dentist and asked her if she was having any problems with her teeth that needed attention. Her face blackened with anger, but she did no more than shake her head without commenting or answering. She realized I was lying, that I was not going to the dentist, and that I only said it to refer indirectly to the subject of her picking at her teeth in front of me while we were eating.

She also would put a finger in her nose and scoop out what was in it. Then she would wipe her finger—in my presence—on anything she could find. It was as if my mother didn't see me sitting right there in front of her, eating with her, and talking to her. (Of course I only talked to her about trivial things anyway.)

Why was my mother doing this? Was it because she had reached a point where my presence and my absence were one and the same? Or was it because I existed and she wanted to show her utter revulsion of this existence? Or was it because she was not ready to expend any effort for my sake when I was present and instead behaved with complete spontaneity and no inhibition whatsoever.

I wonder if my mother no longer acknowledges my existence. Is that why she doesn't treat me with the same kind of respect and consideration she shows others?

Or has time taken away her ability to control her behavior, or rather her desire to control her behavior, bringing her to a state of despair in which she no longer values anything?

I wonder now, I mean now that my father has been murdered, whether she behaved around him the way she behaved around me. Did she renege on the agreement that was forged between them since the beginning of their marriage? Did that anger my father and make him seek revenge in his own way?

I don't ever remember surprising my mother in any unseemly situation, or in an embarrassing situation for me and for her, the way sometimes a child might surprise his mother, in the bathroom for example, or see her naked in the middle of getting dressed, or when she's pulling her stockings all the way up her thighs, or that type of thing. I only remember hearing her tell the story about me when I was a little boy. When she held me in her arms I would put my hand inside her blouse and say, "I want to see!" She would laugh with all her heart. What made her laugh even more was how I would object and pretend to cry because she wouldn't let me put my hand inside her blouse. She would laugh and laugh every time she told the story, even after I grew up. But lately I had started surprising her in ways that shocked me. It wasn't the nature of the events themselves but rather what they signified and indicated. They were a clear indication of a change in my mother, who had always been known for her etiquette and proper behavior. I was afraid this was what most people consider the onset of senility, which made me very sad. I saw her once with the back of her dress caught in her underwear in such a way that the backs of her thighs were showing. I pointed it out to her, and she fixed her dress right in front of me, as simple as that, as though she were all alone and had noticed it herself.

My mother is not that old, really. She's not yet sixty and looks more like she's not yet fifty, which surprises everyone who finds out how old she is. And she doesn't seem to suffer from any illness or weakness of mind or body. She eats well, sleeps well, does all her housework without any help, walks long distances without getting tired, carries groceries by herself all the way home. It's interesting that when she's out she observes the proper etiquette she's known for. I've never heard anyone mention any change in her behavior. It seems that this change has only affected her behavior at home.

I wonder now, I mean now that my father has been murdered, if that change had anything to do with his murder, and if so, what? How was my father murdered and why? Had he been unable to straighten her out or get back at her? Had his attempts to get his revenge backfired on him? What happened? What is this "case of blood revenge" that all the papers mentioned? My father gave up that revenge stuff a long time ago. He had gotten wiser and much more careful.

Had he started leaving the house even more than he used to? Had he decided in his own way to explode the situation he could no longer bear? My father was not capable of bearing the unbearable. It wasn't in him.

How can I possibly uncover these hidden matters, which the newspapers and the police cannot possibly know, regardless of who they interview, without going there myself?

I was rereading my e-mail messages, convincing myself of the necessity to forget all those cautions and obstacles and dangers and go there immediately, without waiting another second, or wasting any more time, when the phone rang. It was around nine o'clock at night. I said to myself, "Finally. It's Salwa." But it was my mother.

Yes! It was my mother herself, calling just like that.

"How could you, Mom? How could you?" I said to her as my blood pressure rose.

"What do you mean, how could I?" she said.

I asked her if it was reasonable that I should find out about my father's murder by chance!

"In the café!" I screamed.

"I found out in the café—by chance—that my own father was murdered!" I blew up at her again. And I also told her that everyone, even the people in the United States and around the world, heard about it except me. I read to her little blurbs from some of the e-mails I received.

"I'm the one affected by his murder, not you. I am his son, not you. I'm the one responsible for avenging him, not you. You—for you this is probably the best day of your life!" I said that with all the strength I could muster and then breathed in deeply and heavily, as though I were breathing in everything around me, as if my lungs hadn't tasted air for ages.

She said (calmly), "I was depending on your uncles and your uncles were depending on me, and it seems we got our lines crossed." She also said, "I understood from one of them that you had been contacted, and when you didn't come, I assumed you were out of the country. I believe most people thought you were out of the country."

While my mother was saying that last sentence, I heard someone in the background telling my mother to say that she kept getting the answering machine and that she doesn't know how to leave a message. She called a hundred times and finally figured he must be away. To say she was sure he must be away.

It was my youngest uncle's voice. I recognized it.

So my mother was calling me from my uncle's house. From Maryam's house. She verified that later when I asked her.

That was Monday night.

Before I told her I was coming right away, I asked her who killed him and why. She said such things could not be discussed on the phone and that she would tell me when I got there.

I told my mother that some of our relatives overseas offered in their e-mails to help in avenging him, and they said that they were ready to do whatever they had to do. She didn't respond, as if she hadn't heard the words. So I asked her if she could hear me. She said *yes*. Then a moment later she added, "There's a government now." She was referring to the fact that the war had ended, the militias had been dissolved, the government institutions had gone back to work, and that it was necessary now to go to court rather than taking matters into your own hands.

After I hung up, I quickly packed a few days' necessities in a small suitcase and went out to the taxi stand near the building where I live. I didn't take my English book with me as I had the two previous times. I did not contact Salwa to tell her that I was going to be away and why, and even when I was in the car I didn't call her. I had my cell phone in my hand, and its battery was fully charged, and all I had to do was press three buttons to bring up her number from the memory and call.

On the way I really felt I wanted to relax and maybe even fall asleep. So I stretched out and yielded to my thoughts, letting them come as they would. I yielded to my dreams and my memories, images from here and fragments from there. One of the things I remembered was the murder of a young man from my family. At the time I was ten years old. My friends and I started having visions of him at night. He would come to me and my friends, wearing his snow white shirt. He would appear to us from the waist up, coming from the dark orange groves on the edge of town. There were red stains on his shirt that were the same in number as the number of bullets that struck him. We were really scared seeing all this, and so we told our parents and other grown-ups. They advised us to speak his name when he appeared. That would make him disappear right away. And they warned us against taking too long to say his name, otherwise it would take him a long time to disappear, and we would be forced to say "Scram!" to him, lest he get angry with us, and a dead person's anger has dreadful consequences. The meaning of "Scram!" here is that we promise to avenge his death as soon as possible. If we don't keep our word, he would keep appearing to us all our lives and might even cause us harm. We told our parents and the other grown-ups later that the victim's brother, who avenged his death shortly after, was taking his time calling out his name on purpose. He wanted to keep him appearing as long as he could because he loved him. At times he would spend hours before saying "Scram!" We were told that he kept on seeing his brother until he got married and had his first son—whom he named after him.

I'm a person who has never believed in ghosts. And I've never believed that the dead have any lingering relationship with things above ground. On the contrary, I am certain that they disintegrate in the soil in which they are buried and become part of it with time. But in spite of this belief, my father appeared to me while I was in the taxi on my way to Zgharta. At times he would pass in front of the car, which nearly hit him, and so I would scream to warn the driver. He was something like those creatures in mythical movies, those animals that circle around their prey, surprising it from a different angle many times, before pouncing on it for the fatal blow. He was wearing a suit and a necktie. His beard was long and grey. And every time he would appear in a different season. Once in the summer, once in the winter.

Those apparitions scared me. No, more than that. I saw in them a sign of impending evil. Suddenly, in the middle of our trip, I asked the driver, "Do you see anyone?"

He asked what I meant, and I didn't know what to say to him. It was impossible for me to explain to him that my father was appearing to me and was walking around outside our car on his own two feet, and that he had no problem keeping up with the speed of the car, because he moved at the speed of thought. Yes! At the speed of thought my father circled around the car that was going as fast as it could on that part of the Beirut–Tripoli highway, in Haalaat, just before Byblos, where the Lebanese Forces wanted to build an airport during the Lebanese war. It was a clear night, the moon was radiant, with just a few scattered clouds in the sky.

I couldn't find a way to change the subject and make the driver forget the question that I had just asked him, except to ask him another question.

"Have you ever heard of anyone who was not informed of his own father's murder? Neither by his mother, nor his uncles, nor his friends, nor anyone?"

The driver answered, "So then how did he find out?"

"And he was his only son!" I said.

"How did he find out?" he said.

"By chance," I said.

"Where does he live? Outside the country? Did he move?"

"No! In Beirut!" I said.

"Are you sure he's his father?"

Suddenly I felt extremely tired, and I felt that if I were to answer him, even with one word, it would take more effort than I was capable of exerting. But I said to him anyway, after I paused a little and took a deep breath to assemble my strength, "Definitely! Definitely!"